D0191087

THE Closest Thing TO Flying

GILL LEWIS

OXFORD
UNIVERSITY PRESS

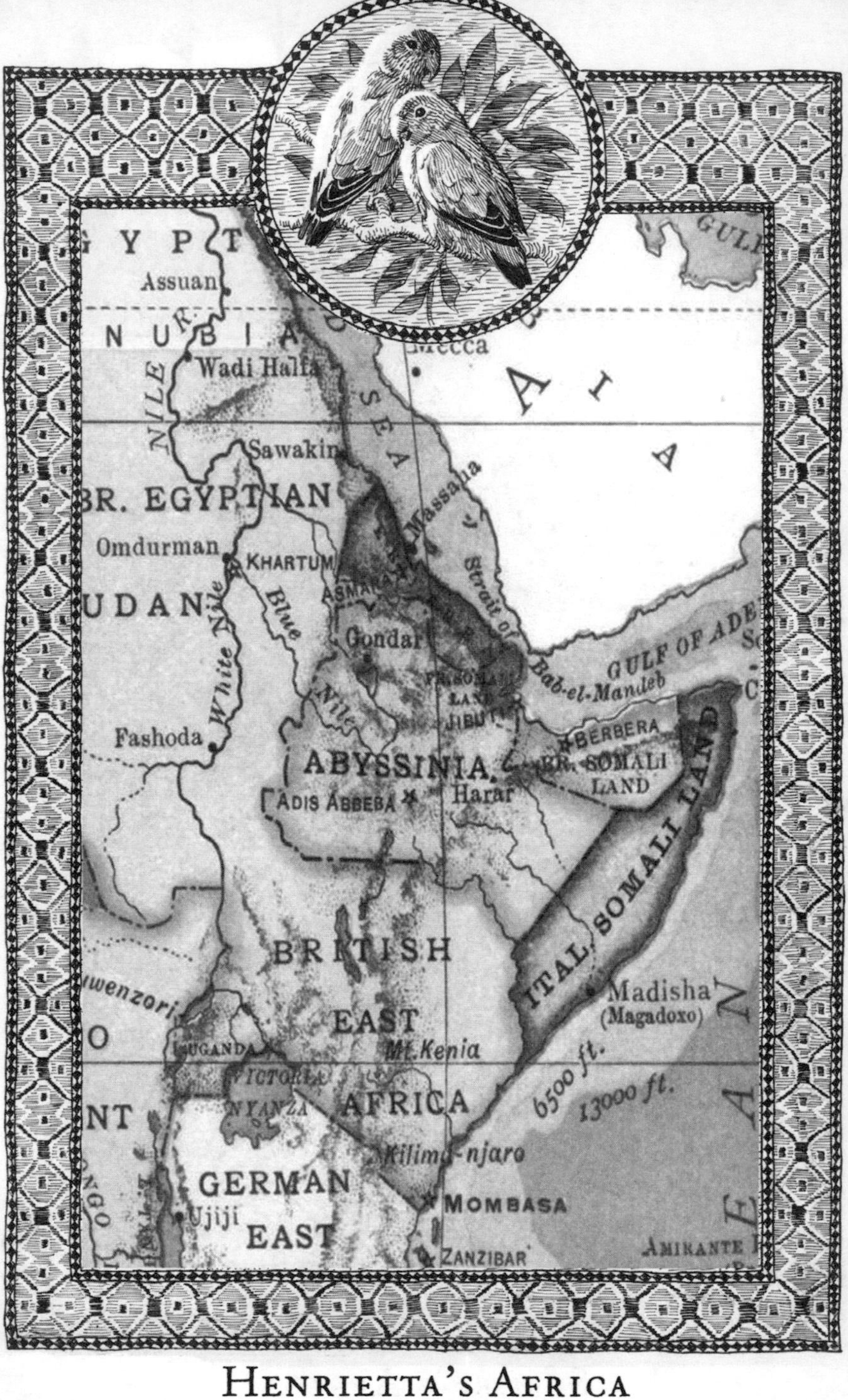

HENRIETTA'S AFRICA

SEMIRA'S AFRICA

Chapter 1

Semira wasn't sure what it was about the hat that made her stop and look.

Maybe it was the bird.

She had seen a bird like this before.

Some time ago.

Hot sun. Blue sky. Red earth. Wide puddle. Green bird.

Green bird.

The bird on the hat was real. It was small and parrot-like, with emerald-green feathers and a red coral-coloured beak. It was stuffed and positioned, its wings in flight as if trying to escape.

Maybe that's why she had stopped.

Or maybe it was because the hat had been

crushed. It was a mangled mess of felt and wire. The velvet flowers and leaves had been ripped and torn. Maybe it was seeing something so beautiful that had been deliberately destroyed and battered almost beyond recognition. Yet the bird remained untouched. It was still perfect, but held by a strand of wire so fine as to be almost invisible, its beak open in some desperate, silent cry.

She leaned in for a closer look.

'Twenty quid, love.'

Semira looked up.

The man behind the stall yawned and drank from his mug of coffee. 'It's Victorian. Over a hundred years old,' he said. 'The real thing.'

Semira looked back at the hat. She only had the change in her pocket from the ten-pound note Robel had given her to buy a set of saucepans at the second-hand market. She'd bought them cheap as they had lost their non-stick coating, and she had four pounds left over.

Still, it wasn't enough to buy the hat.

She wasn't thinking of buying it anyway.

Was she?

The man took another swig of coffee.

The hat sat among the rest of the bric-a-brac at Ron's stall. Ron and his brother were the clearance people. They bought up and sold the contents of the houses of people who had died when there were no relatives to come for the belongings. Semira had been with Robel to pick up a microwave oven from Ron only yesterday. There wasn't much on the stall today: a china dog, a half set of teacups, a copper ash bucket, and a poker for a fire. No one in London had real fires these days did they?

And then there was the hat.

The hat with the bird.

'What sort is it?' asked Semira.

'Eh?'

'What sort of bird?' said Semira.

'Dunno,' said Ron. 'Wassit matter?'

The woman at the next stall leaned over to him. 'You'd be rubbish on *Antiques Roadshow*, Ron.' She turned to Semira. 'He'll let you have it for ten quid, love.'

Ron scowled. 'It's Victorian. It came from that mad professor's house.'

'It's a pile of junk,' said the woman. 'You couldn't wear it. He'll let you have it for a fiver, love. He hasn't sold anything all day.' She chuckled, clearly enjoying herself.

Semira reached into her pocket and held out the four pound coins.

Ron placed his mug down with a thump. He turned to the woman. 'I've not seen you sell anything today. Sell your own stuff.'

'Aw, c'mon. You can see the girl wants the hat. You'll never get rid of it. You'll end up chucking it away.'

Ron rolled his eyes and picked up the hat, holding it out to Semira.

'And the box it comes in,' said the woman.

Semira hadn't noticed the box it was sitting on. A cylindrical hatbox covered in faded black velvet.

'That's separate,' said Ron.

'You can't do that,' said the woman. 'It's against consumer rights, that is. They go together.'

Ron opened the hatbox, shoved the hat inside, handed it to Semira, and snatched the coins from her hand.

The woman chuckled again. 'Reckon you should employ me, Ron. I'd clear your stall in a day.'

Semira balanced the bag of saucepans on top of the hatbox and left them bickering. It was a huge hatbox and much heavier than it looked. What had she done? What was she thinking? Why had she even bought it?

Robel would be furious if he found out.

She and Mama were never allowed to buy anything for themselves or to keep any of the money. They had to give any money they had to him.

It would be hard to hide the hatbox from Robel.

Maybe she should just take it back, or throw it away.

But there was something about it.

What was it about the emerald-green bird that had caught her eye?

Semira hugged the hatbox against her chest and kept on walking.

And all she could think is that she wanted to find out why.

CHAPTER 2

The new house Robel had found for them was even smaller than the last. And there seemed to be more people in this house too. Most of them were young men. People never seemed to stay long in the houses Robel found. Semira guessed some were Sudanese and Syrian. There was a Congolese woman and her son in the last house, but no one else from Eritrea like Semira and her mother. Semira sometimes wondered if Robel did it on purpose so that her mother had no one else to talk to. No one else she knew apart from Robel and Mama spoke the Tigrinya language of Eritrea, and Mama couldn't speak English. At the last house, he had stopped her from going to church, saying it was too far to walk on her own. At least Semira and Mama had their own room together this time. And this room had a lock. Someone had stolen her trainers in the last house and she couldn't go to school until Robel bought new ones for her. Despite the lock, Mama still pushed the bed against the door before they went to sleep.

Semira sighed.

A new school tomorrow too. It was the beginning of the summer term and she would be going into another year seven. Everyone would know each other already. Friendship groups would already have been made.

Still, at least she was going to school. There had been times when she didn't go to a school at all.

Semira didn't want to go back to the house, but there was nowhere else to go, and it was cold too. It was an April day of blue sky and clear bright sunlight, bringing everything into sharp focus. She stopped on the bridge to watch the Thames slide beneath her. It churned and swirled, the deep undercurrents rising to the surface in spiralling eddies. Maybe she was like the river, she thought, always moving, never stopping, and leaving places and friends behind. She used to make an effort with each new place, each new school. But it made the leaving harder. She knew she would always be the one moving on and moving through.

She pulled her hood up against the chill wind blowing along the river and headed back to the house. She walked past the doughnut stall and her stomach rumbled at the sticky scent of sugar. It gnawed at her with the guilt of spending the change on the hat. Four pounds. She could have bought food for a couple of days with that. She stopped at the house next to the laundrette, pushed her key in the lock of the front door, and let herself in.

There were people crammed into the front room watching football on a big screen. Semira kept her head down and walked quickly past, but she heard a shout behind her.

'Semira!'

It was Robel's voice.

She hurried up the stairs to the small room she shared with Mama. She pushed open the door, but Robel followed her into the room.

'What's that?' said Robel.

'I bought the pans,' said Semira holding up the bag.

'I mean what's this?' said Robel, taking the hatbox from her. He looked inside and pulled out the hat. The corners of his mouth turned down in distaste. 'What is *this*?'

Semira's mother stood up and looked between Semira and Robel.

'Nothing,' said Semira. 'I found it.'

'Found it?' said Robel. He took a step closer to her. 'How much did you pay for it?'

'Not much,' Semira mumbled.

Robel slipped into the Tigrinya language for Mama to understand. 'I give you money and you can't look after it. How are you going to eat? How are you going to buy clothes? Do I have to do everything for you? How would you survive without me?'

Semira looked at her feet.

'I look after you, and this is how you repay

me.' Robel threw the hatbox across the room where it split on the hard edge of the small table. He threw the hat after it.

'I'm sorry, Robel,' whispered Semira. She glanced at Mama, but Mama's eyes were downcast.

Robel paced across the small patch of carpet to the window and looked out. 'You must call me Papa, remember?'

'Yes, Robel,' mumbled Semira.

Robel slammed his hand on the table. 'What did I say?'

'Yes, Papa,' said Semira.

'Don't forget it,' he snapped. 'Our application to settle here is going through. If the immigration officers find out we have lied, we are all in trouble.'

'Yes, Papa,' repeated Semira.

Robel walked back to the door. He nodded at Semira's mother. 'Come,' he said. 'We are lucky. I know a man who said he will give you work in the hotel tonight. We are meeting him soon.'

Semira's mother stood up and looked at Semira. She turned her hand, miming the action of locking the door.

Semira nodded and watched them leave then turned the key in the lock behind them. Her stomach rumbled but there was no food to eat. The room was cold too, and empty without Mama. This was a new part of London and Semira didn't know anyone.

She was alone.

Again.

She crossed the room to pick up the hat and the broken hatbox. She tried to push the split halves together, but something was caught in the way.

At the base of the hatbox was a hidden flat compartment containing a pair of very small leather gloves. But there was something else wedged in too.

Tucked into the glove layer was a book. It was hard to pull out, but Semira gently eased it with her fingers. It was a brown cloth-bound book, with a long feather inked on the cover. The ink had bled into the cloth, but Semira could read the words, *The Feather Diaries*.

A diary.

Semira looked behind her as if she felt someone was watching her. A diary was personal wasn't it? Private?

But surely if it had been written over a hundred years ago, the writer of the diary would be dead by now.

It wouldn't matter if she read some of it.

Would it?

After all, she had nothing else to read, and it would be hours before Mama would return.

Semira climbed into bed and pulled the duvet up around her.

Her fingers hovered over the cloth cover.

She bit her lip, hesitating for a moment.

Then she turned the page and began to read . . .

CHAPTER 3

The Feather Diaries

Tuesday 12th May, 1891

Dear Friend,

Are you there?
Are you real?
I feel so lonely that I need someone to talk to.
I hope you do not mind me addressing you as a friend.
It's a silly fancy of mine, I know.
You can't answer me.
But somehow, addressing you as 'dear diary' makes me feel even lonelier.

13

Besides, diaries are for self-indulgent thoughts. I need someone to listen to me. I need to tell someone my story.

Maybe you are real. Maybe you are listening.

I'm not even sure how to write to you. Mother would instruct me to use formal language and write neatly as if I were writing a letter to one of the Society Ladies she entertains. However, I would rather write to you as a friend and share my thoughts as friends do.

But I am getting ahead of myself.

I should introduce myself.

My name is Henrietta Margaret Waterman.

I was born on 12th May 1879 and today is my twelfth birthday.

I live in the city of London, a short stroll from Regent's Park, with my father, mother, and sister Lettie.

Father is a feather merchant. He owns a warehouse on Cutler Street and it is filled with the feathers and skins of birds from around the world. Plumes of all colours of the rainbow are stacked high; hummingbirds from South America, egret feathers from the Everglades, golden pheasants from the Far East. Father says trade is booming, and that the milliners who make the feather-topped hats cannot make them fast enough.

Mother runs the household. She organizes Father's diary and says that good business requires knowing the right people in the right places. She knows the most fashionable ladies who love to purchase the rarest of bird skins and feathers from Father's warehouse.

Lettie is my little sister and is quite the bonniest child I know. You would love her too. She has bright-blue eyes and golden ringlets and can always raise a smile from anyone.

I have mouse-brown hair and a face that Mother describes as not unpleasant, but rather plain. My governess, Miss Spinks, says the most beautiful flowers are always late to bloom and that their blooms last the longest. I hope she is right, but Miss Spinks always says nice things to cheer people up when they are feeling glum.

Lettie and I share the nursery. Miss Spinks and the maid share one of the attic rooms and Cook has the other. Cook sleeps on her own on account of her snoring. Even Lettie and I can hear her through the ceiling above our room.

Mrs Tindall, our housekeeper, comes to the house at six sharp every morning and leaves at six in the evening. She doesn't live with us because her husband is bedridden after falling into the path of a runaway horse and carriage. She has a daughter, although I have never seen her.

Mother would like a butler, but Father says good butlers are expensive and hard to find these days and that Mrs Tindall will have to do.

I suppose my life has been quite unremarkable until today when my whole world has been turned upside down.

Who would have thought a bird on a hat could change everything? But it has. And how quickly things can change. Only this morning I was admiring Mother's new hat, a present from Father. She declared it to be the most beautiful one she has ever seen. It is crafted with velvet and lace to resemble a wild forest. There is a gay little emerald-green bird, like a small parrot, in the pose of flight. Father said the bird came all the way from Abyssinia, far, far away in the Horn of Africa.

Mother said these hats celebrate the glory of God's creation, and that it pleased God for us to adorn ourselves with His work.

I thought that too, until the extraordinary meeting of today.

And now, all I can see are the empty forests, and rows and rows of murdered birds for our own pleasure.

I cannot discuss this with Mother or Father because they would most certainly disapprove. Father's business depends upon this endless supply of feathers. I can't tell Lettie because she's only five and won't understand. The only person I could trust would be Miss Spinks, but it's precisely because she's not here that I find myself in this sorry mess.

Miss Spinks was called away late last night to care for her sick father in Oxford and so she couldn't be here to take me for a birthday tea in Town today. Mother had already accepted an invitation to visit the wife of the Mayor and present her with the bright skin of a fiery-throated hummingbird, and so Father called on Aunt Katherine to accompany me into Town instead.

That's when it all began.

Now, sitting here in bed, writing by the light of this lamp, I feel so confused that I barely know my own mind.

You see, the bird on the hat changed everything. Everything.

And I know that nothing can ever be the same again.

Semira put the diary down and climbed out of bed to pick up the hat. She curled back under the duvet and stared at the bird. The bird was over a hundred years old. But she had definitely seen a bird like this before.

She tried to reach for a memory that stayed hidden from her somewhere in the shadows.

Hot sun. Blue sky. Red earth. Wide puddle. Green bird.

A wide puddle.

A green bird drinking at the water's edge.

And a paper boat.

A paper boat floating across a vast puddle-sea.

A man's voice. Deep and gentle: 'Godspeed

little boat. Godspeed.'

Someone was blowing the boat, a warm breath of wind carrying it on small ripples across the sea to safety.

Semira tried to hold onto the memory. She tried to reach through and see who was blowing the boat, but the bird at the water's edge became startled and the memory spun away and blurred in a flurry of wing beats.

She sighed and traced her finger from the bird's beak over the curve of its head and body, gently touching the outstretched wings. Many years ago another girl her age had sat looking at this bird.

Something about it had changed her life.

Semira wondered if she and the diary were somehow connected, as if her whole future was bound up within its pages.

Maybe this small green bird could unlock the secrets of Semira's past.

Maybe it could even change Semira's whole life too.

CHAPTER 4

Semira picked the diary up again and held it against her chest. Outside the sun was setting behind the rooftops, but Semira didn't want to switch on the light. It felt as if Henrietta were living and breathing in the room with her. She didn't want to break the moment. 'Hello Henrietta,' she whispered. She sighed and put the book down. What was she doing, talking to a book? It had been written over a hundred years ago, by a girl her age, but so different from her. Yet, strangely, it felt as if Henrietta was talking just to her.

Semira decided to put the book away and read it slowly, one entry at a time. She slipped the book beneath the pile of clean clothes in her drawer, and placed the hat on the windowsill.

She curled up in bed, wrapping the duvet around her, watching the evening darken behind the hat, silhouetting the bird against the sky. The bird seemed to be trapped by the wire, frantically trying to escape into the night.

She tried to reach again for the memory. Hot sun. Blue sky. Red earth. Wide puddle. Green bird. She stared at the bird as if it could somehow take her back there, but her eyelids felt heavy and she let sleep take her down, down down, until she was lying deep inside a paper boat.

'*Godspeed little boat. Godspeed.*'

The paper boat rose and fell, rocking on the water. Up and down. Up and down. But the wind was changing and soon the waves began to rise. Semira clutched at the side of the boat. Water was seeping through the paper hull. She wasn't alone any more, because the boat was crammed with people; men, women, children, and babies. As Semira looked around she couldn't tell if they were alive or dead, but they were all wearing hats with long feathers. Robel was in the boat too holding up a cage, and inside the cage was the green bird. And the green bird was her mother. Robel said they were all going to drown and it was all Semira's fault. Semira could see the cage door was wide open, but Mama stayed on the perch. *Fly, Mama fly*, called Semira, but she wouldn't move. Semira wanted to set her free, but Robel said it was too late and he threw the cage into the waves and then all Semira could hear was Mama calling for help.

'Semira . . . Semira . . . Semira.'

Semira woke with a start and a sharp intake of breath. 'Mama?'

It was dark in the room, with just the orange glow of streetlight through the window. She didn't know how long she had been asleep.

'Semira!' Soft knocking. 'It's me, Mama. Let me come in.'

Semira unlocked the door, let her in, and locked it again.

Mama pushed the bed against the door and stroked Semira's forehead. 'Go back to bed, child. It's late.'

Semira climbed back in bed and felt her mother curl up beside her. She usually slept on a thin mattress on the floor, but Semira was glad of her company tonight.

'Mama?'

'Yes child?'

'Why do we let Robel tell us what to do?' said Semira.

'Robel brought us here. If they find we have lied to try to stay here, we might be sent back to Eritrea. Robel is trying to sort it for us.'

'But he doesn't let you have any money, yet you earned it.'

Mama sighed. 'It is not that simple. Robel knows the system. He speaks English. He can fill in the forms. He can get things from the shops for us.'

'I speak English, Mama,' said Semira. 'I can buy what we need.'

'We need Robel, Semira. We cannot go back home. We cannot. Don't ask me more about this.'

Semira listened to the sound of Mama's

breathing slow down and settle as she began sliding into sleep.

'Mama?'

'Yes child?'

'The bird on the hat. I have seen one like it before,' said Semira.

Mama stayed silent.

'There was a puddle and a paper boat and someone was blowing it across the water.'

'You remember that?' said Mama. 'That was before we came to England. You could only have been five years old.'

Semira locked her fingers into her mother's. They had arrived in England when Semira was seven years old. All her mother came with was Semira and an old red carpetbag of belongings. Robel had brought them across the desert and the sea to be here. Semira tried not to remember the journey and the camps they had stayed in, and Mama never spoke of it.

'There was a man,' said Semira. 'There was a man blowing the paper boat. He had a deep voice. He said *Godspeed*.'

Mama didn't say anything but Semira

became aware Mama was holding her breath.

'That man,' said Semira. 'The man who blew the boat. It wasn't Robel, was it?'

'No,' said Mama. 'It was not.'

Semira could feel her mother's hot tears soak through her nightshirt. 'Mama? Who was he?'

'Hush, Semira,' said Mama. 'Get some sleep. You have school tomorrow.'

But Semira didn't fall asleep.

She kept thinking about the man who blew the paper boat.

She stayed awake long into the night.

Chapter 5

The new school was a forty-minute walk from the house. Semira had walked there at the weekend to make sure she knew the way. She sat on her bed and pulled on the school shirt and black trousers Robel had picked up at a second-hand uniform shop. The grey blazer was too big but it was clean at least. She doubted she would stay long enough at this school to grow out of it.

Mama braided Semira's hair. 'Be careful today. Stay away from troublemakers.'

Semira nodded.

She straightened Semira's collar. 'And don't go upsetting Robel. Remember, we may all need to see the immigration officer soon. You might be asked questions. You know what to say?'

'Yes, Mama,' said Semira. 'I pretend Robel is my father. I say he was a journalist and tried to stand up against the government. If we go back he will be imprisoned and life will be too difficult for us.'

'Good. Now go downstairs and get some breakfast.'

'But Robel wasn't a journalist was he?' said Semira.

'No,' said Mama. 'Now enough questions. There is some flatbread in a blue box on our shelf.'

The house was quiet in the morning. Some people were out on nightshift work and others were still in bed. Semira could hear snoring from several rooms. She let herself into the kitchen to see one of the young men making coffee and Robel sitting at the table eating flatbread. Semira glanced at Robel. She noticed he had red eyes from a late night out. His paunch showed between the stretched buttons on his shirt. He stared at her as she opened the cupboard for the blue box.

'It's empty,' Robel muttered.

Semira opened it and looked inside. 'Is there any other food?'

'You should have saved that money yesterday,' he said, wiping his mouth with the back of his hand. 'You can't eat a hat. You'll have to go hungry. It'll teach you not to waste money.' He stood up and left the room, slamming the door.

Semira felt hot angry tears well up.

'Here.' The young man handed her some kitchen towel.

'Thank you,' she said. She wiped her eyes but couldn't ignore the loud rumble from her stomach. She hadn't eaten since lunchtime the day before.

'You're new here,' the man said. 'My name is Abdul.'

'Semira,' said Semira.

Abdul reached up to his shelf in the cupboard. 'You can't go to school on an empty stomach.' He pulled two pieces of bread from a bag and put them in the toaster.

Semira inhaled the smell of warm toast. 'Have you got enough to share?'

'I've got plenty, so you must eat,' insisted Abdul. 'I have a sister back home who is your age. God willing, I hope someone is looking after her too.'

'Thank you,' said Semira.

Abdul nodded his head at the door. 'Is that your father?'

Semira looked down at the floor. She hated lying. Besides, it was obvious she and Robel looked nothing like each other. She was tall for her age with long limbs and dark-brown skin. She had wide cheekbones and wide-set eyes. Robel was short, with a paunch. His face was long and thin and his skin was paler than hers, and tinged an unhealthy ash-grey.

Abdul drank some coffee. 'I'm sorry. Too many questions. We all have our own secrets and stories to tell.'

'Have you been here long?' asked Semira.

Abdul shrugged his shoulders. 'I've been here since eternity and have not been here long enough.'

Semira smiled. She knew exactly what he meant.

Abdul pulled the hot toast from the toaster and pushed a pot of jam across to Semira. 'Help yourself.'

Semira spread the jam thinly, reaching all four corners of the toast. She took a bite and chewed slowly, savouring the taste.

Abdul gave a little bow. 'Take care, Semira. If you want to store your food on my shelf to keep it safe, you are welcome to.'

'Thank you, Abdul.' Semira shouldered her bag and headed towards the new school.

She wondered what this new school would be like. The last school had pupils like her who had been forced to leave their homes and countries, and so fitting in was no problem. It was easy to become invisible. But other schools were new to refugees. Semira was used to those too, from the over-friendly pupils to the rude ones who shouted insults. It didn't bother Semira any more. She had learned to build a shell around herself. She could almost see it and touch it. When bullies found indifference, they became bored and left her alone. When kind people found coolness, they turned away. It was easier to stay distant. Nobody got hurt.

She stood at the front gates and watched other pupils filing past her. She wished Mama had come with her. She always had to do these first days on her own. Semira walked through the gates, expanding her shell around her as she went.

CHAPTER 6

The morning began with form-tutor time. The teacher took Semira to the side and introduced her to two girls. 'We have a buddy system here,' she said. 'Holly and Chloe have offered to show you around and help you get to know the school this week.'

Semira smiled at the two girls, but inwardly wanted to be left alone. School buddies were usually the confident outgoing pupils, the sort that ran the school council, the sort that saw the introduction of a new pupil as their new pet project. Holly and Chloe looked that sort.

Holly pushed her hair back and leaned against a table. 'Have you got your timetable?'

Semira nodded and unfolded the piece

of paper the teacher had given her with the printed timetable.

Holly looked over her shoulder. 'That's an old one. You can get the updated one on your phone. Has the school set up your school account and given you a password yet?'

'My phone's broken,' Semira lied. She didn't want to admit she didn't have a phone and that she'd never had one.

Chloe laughed. 'You can't be as bad as Holly. She gets the prize for the most broken phones. That's her third phone this year.'

Chloe held up her phone and sniggered. 'I dropped my last one down the toilet. Mum went mental. She said I had to use some of my birthday money to pay for it.'

The bell rang and Holly shouldered her bag. 'Science,' she groaned, leading the way to the science block.

Chloe walked alongside Semira. 'Is it true you came over here on one of those boats?'

Holly stopped to jab Chloe in the ribs. 'Chloe!'

Semira kept her eyes fixed on the ground.

'That was years ago,' she said. 'I've been here since I was seven. We've moved from a different part of London.'

'Where d'you live now?' asked Chloe.

'Not far,' said Semira, trying to be vague. 'The other side of the river.'

'That's nearer to the Academy School,' said Holly. 'Sorry you ended up at this dump. Mum and Dad wanted me to go to the Academy, but there weren't enough places.'

'Same,' said Chloe. 'So how come you ended up here?'

Semira shrugged her shoulders and hoped they'd stop asking questions.

The science block was a separate building at the back of the school and Semira followed Chloe and Holly to one of the classrooms on the top floor. The other students had already taken their seats and Semira could only see a spare seat at the front of the class next to a boy with red hair.

Chloe grabbed a spare stool and made space for Semira to sit between her and Holly. 'It wouldn't be fair to make you sit next to the

Bird Nerd on your first day.'

Semira frowned. 'Who?'

Chloe nodded her head in the direction of the boy with red hair. 'Him. Patrick.'

Semira glanced over at Patrick. He had been looking at her, but he quickly turned away.

'You want to watch out for him,' said Holly.

'Why?' asked Semira.

'He's harmless,' said Chloe. 'He's just . . . he's just . . . '

'. . . he's just Patrick,' laughed Holly. 'A bit odd. Intense. You know the type.'

Semira opened her textbook and pretended to read. Trying to work out the friendships at a new school never got any easier. To survive you had to keep your head down, try and be the same as everyone else, and fit in.

Chloe and Holly steered Semira through maths and then English. By the end of the morning she didn't mind them so much. They were friendly, and to Semira's relief, they wanted to talk more about themselves and others in the school than ask questions about her.

'You can sit with us at lunch,' said Chloe.

'The food's actually OK most days.'

'I'll find you later,' said Semira. 'I've got to see my tutor.' It was a lie, but it was becoming easier to lie. Robel hadn't filled in the forms to claim for free school meals and she didn't want to admit she didn't have any money.

Instead, at lunchtime, Semira made her way to the library. She was relieved to find the school did have a library. It was just about the only place she could be on her own without feeling awkward, and libraries were usually warm inside. At the last school, the librarian had a secret stash of biscuits she sometimes brought out at break. There were computers too, so Semira could do her homework. Robel had a laptop and a phone, but he never let Semira or Mama use them.

Semira sat in a corner seat and logged on to a computer, trying to ignore her hunger pangs. She sat staring at the screen. Her mind went back to the bird on the hat, the same type of bird she had seen drinking from a puddle. Henrietta's father had said it was from Abyssinia. She typed in the word *Abyssinia*.

The screen filled with a map of the Horn of Africa and showed that part of Ethiopia was once named Abyssinia. The thin strip of country against the coastline above Ethiopia was Eritrea, the homeland of her mother, the country she was born in but couldn't remember.

Next, Semira typed in the words *green bird Abyssinia*. An image appeared showing the same bird on the hat. The bird was an Abyssinian Lovebird. The male had a block of bright-red feathers on its forehead while the female was all green. Both had bright-red bills. So the bird on the hat was a female. She had seen this bird before. It pulled and pulled on her memory.

'What's that then?'

Semira looked around. She hadn't noticed Patrick looking over her shoulder. He peered more closely at the screen, pushing up glasses that kept slipping down his nose.

She turned back to the screen again. 'Abyssinian Lovebird,' she said.

'Cool,' said Patrick. He pulled over a chair

and sat next to her, leaning his elbows on the table. 'Thought so.'

Semira ignored him and continued reading.

'You're Semira aren't you?' said Patrick. 'I'm Patrick.'

Semira kept her eyes on the screen, scrolling down the site, hoping Patrick would leave her alone.

'Have you seen one before?' said Patrick. 'In the wild, I mean?'

Semira nodded her head.

'Cool,' said Patrick. 'Are you a twitcher too?'

'A what?' said Semira.

'A twitcher,' said Patrick. 'Do you go birdwatching too?'

Semira shrugged her shoulders. She didn't want to encourage conversation. 'No. I saw one years ago.'

'Where was that?' said Patrick.

'Eritrea,' said Semira.

'Cool,' said Patrick. 'I've only seen those birds in cages. It's not right, though, to keep them in cages. They don't last long.'

Semira turned to look at him. 'Why not?'

'When they realize they can't escape, they just slowly give up and die,' said Patrick. 'Imagine being stuck with no way out. What would you have to live for?'

Semira's hands hovered over the keyboard. She shut her eyes tightly against tears that had formed so suddenly and unexpectedly.

Her thoughts felt scrambled. All she could think of was Mama stuck in the house with Robel, and the dead bird on the hat trapped by invisible wire.

She logged out, grabbed her bag, and left.

'Semira!' called Patrick.

But Semira didn't stop. She wanted to get away as far as possible.

'Semira!' called Patrick again.

She heard his footsteps running after her and then his hand pulling her arm. She spun around, furious that she couldn't stop her tears from falling. 'Leave me alone.'

'I'm sorry,' said Patrick. 'I didn't mean . . .'

Semira pulled her arm away and ran.

She'd been stupid to let her guard down.

CHAPTER 6

No good ever came from it.

Ever.

But Patrick had just broken through her shell.

CHAPTER 7

Semira sat through afternoon lessons, and then left school as soon as the final bell rang. She ran back to the house. She and Mama were like caged birds, she thought. They were let out to fly for a little while, but Robel controlled everything they did. They couldn't escape. They couldn't talk to anyone. They were stuck. For ever.

Henrietta hadn't had anyone to talk to either. Yet it seemed as if she were talking to Semira. What was it about the bird? Maybe it did offer an escape.

Robel and Mama were both out when she returned to the house, so Semira locked herself in her room and opened the diary again.

41

Henrietta's thoughts had spilled out over the pages, the inked words looping and swirling across decades, spanning a whole century.

Semira tried to imagine Henrietta bent over the diary scribbling hurriedly, writing to try to find sense within her world. Henrietta, it seemed, came from a wealthy family. She had a family and enough food to eat and a house to live in. What could possibly be so hard for her?

Yet she sounded just as lonely as Semira felt.

Semira pulled the duvet up around her and read on.

So dear friend, maybe if I tell you everything as it happens, then you can be a trusted witness I can call upon.

I had to wait until after luncheon for Aunt Katherine to arrive to take me for a birthday tea. Mother does not approve of Aunt Katherine and I too am a little nervous of her. She is Father's youngest sister and nearer to my age than Father's. She will turn nineteen next month.

I have met her only on a few occasions. The

last, being the wake held after Great-Uncle Gerald's funeral. Aunt Katherine wore a pink flower in her hair. It looked so gay against the sombre black attire of other folk. I remember Mother making small talk and saying Uncle Gerald was now in a better place. Then Aunt Katherine laughed loudly and said six foot beneath the earth was the best place for Uncle Gerald and she hoped maggots were already eating his eyeballs. Mother felt quite faint and needed smelling salts after that.

So I took a back step as Aunt Katherine swept into the parlour. Father seemed a little on edge too. Aunt Katherine reminds me of a mare Father once bought. Beautiful but dangerous. Like her, it had a mane of wild black hair. I fear the poor beast was shot, as no man could ever tame it.

Aunt Katherine tapped her foot in impatience. 'The cab is waiting.'

Mother fussed with my ribbons and tightened my corset. 'Breathe in dear!'

I did breathe in, but I am of rather stout features like Father and thick-waisted too. I do not possess the waifish figure of my cousins. Marybelle has an eighteen-inch waist, so Mother often tells me.

'Henrietta, greet your aunt,' said Mother when she had finished with me.

I curtsied but felt too shy to speak.

'It's a wonder she can speak at all with her corset pulled so tight,' said Aunt Katherine. She turned to me and flashed a wicked smile. 'Though I hope she doesn't loosen it in the cab. I dread to think what might happen to all that trapped wind!'

Lettie exploded into giggles, and I went bright red and had to stifle a laugh.

Mother glared at Aunt Katherine. 'I don't care for vulgar talk. It is most unladylike.'

'Oh Josephine,' chided Aunt Katherine. 'Everyone breaks wind, even the Queen.'

Lettie could not stop giggling until Mother told her to go to her room.

I was a little in awe of Aunt Katherine. I have never heard anyone stand up to Mother before.

'Well, come along,' said Aunt Katherine to me. 'We can't keep the Duchess of Portland waiting.'

'The Duchess of Portland?' exclaimed Mother.

I looked at Mother. She was clearly annoyed that Aunt Katherine had the Duchess's acquaintance and that she did not.

Father was surprised too. 'What is your business with her?'

'Oh you know,' said Aunt Katherine. 'It's women's talk. I'm sure, dear brother, that you would find it most frightfully dull.'

Father bristled. Aunt Katherine was mocking him. I didn't realize it at the time but this was a clear indication of the day to come. The atmosphere prickled like the air before a storm.

I gathered my embroidery and followed Aunt Katherine to the waiting cab. Mrs Tindall hurried after us and pressed a small cake box into Aunt Katherine's hand. 'A little something you might fancy later, Miss Waterman. I wouldn't want you to miss out.'

'Thank you Mrs Tindall,' said Aunt Katherine, 'you know I have a fondness for your cake.' She gave a little wink as if a secret passed between friends, yet I can see no reason for their acquaintance, for Mrs Tindall is much beneath her.

Aunt Katherine turned to me as the horse set off at a fast trot. 'I'm afraid birthday tea is cancelled. I have an important meeting to attend and you will have to come too. Besides, you are now twelve and it is time for you to look beyond the nursery walls.'

I must have looked a little alarmed because Aunt Katherine tried to put me at ease. 'We are on our way to meet with the Duchess of Portland and some rather interesting women. Tell me, does the group called the Fur, Fin, and Feather Folk mean anything to you?'

I shook my head.

Aunt Katherine smiled. 'I thought not. Well, soon you are going to find out, though I am quite certain your father and mother would be horrified to know.'

We travelled through London via Piccadilly and stopped outside a rather grand building on Jermyn Street, and I followed Aunt Katherine between the tall columns of the entrance and into a lift that clanked and whirred and took us up and up into the heart of the building.

'This is the headquarters of the Royal Society

for the Prevention of Cruelty to Animals,' said Aunt Katherine. 'And we have been offered a room to discuss the future of birds.'

Aunt Katherine and I were led into a rather dark room that smelled of wood polish and cigar smoke. It seemed like a room that was more comfortable with the company of men than women. Several ladies sat around a mahogany table sipping tea and eating delicate sandwiches.

'Kitty darling, so glad you could make it,' said a rather tall, glamorous woman embracing Aunt Katherine.

'I wouldn't miss it for the world, Winnie,' said Aunt Katherine. She turned to me. 'Henrietta, let me introduce you to Her Grace, the Duchess of Portland.'

I curtsied but didn't say a word.

Aunt Katherine then introduced me to Etta Smith and Eliza Phillips from the Fur, Fin, and Feather Folk. Eliza was much the older of the two women and had a warm smile, whereas Etta was much younger and sharpish, and looked at me as if she could see right into me.

'And this is Georgina Lewis,' said Aunt Katherine, introducing me to another woman. 'Georgina is a surgeon from Edinburgh. She is also a member of the group.'

I just stared at the woman in front of me. She didn't look that much older than Aunt Katherine. There was an easy confidence about her that I'd seen in friends' brothers, and yet also a warmth too. I couldn't help wonder if I had misheard. I have never heard of a woman doctor before.

There was a knock at the door and another woman entered and stood a little nervously waiting to be introduced.

Etta Smith greeted her. 'Thank you for coming all the way from Manchester.' She turned to us all. 'Please let me introduce Emily Williamson, the founder of the Society for the Protection of Birds. It is our aim to join our two groups today and stop the mass slaughter of birds.'

I must have looked confused because the Duchess looked across at me. 'I apologize. Maybe we should explain our aims to the younger member here.'

Etta Smith nodded and turned to me. 'My

dear, have you ever wondered about the feathers in women's hats?'

'Why yes,' I said. 'The birds in my father's warehouse come from all around the world.'

'Really?' said Etta Smith. Her expression was quite sour. 'And your mother wears these feathers?'

'Oh yes,' I said. 'The new hat Father gave her is decorated with a bird all the way from Abyssinia. The green feathers are quite exquisite.'

Etta Smith did not seem to share in my appreciation. She said, 'And what will your mother wear when there are no birds left, when all have been killed for hats?'

I was a little taken aback. 'But Father trades in feathers. He says there are so many birds.'

'And what does he know?' said Etta Smith. 'The dodo is long extinct. The great auk went extinct here in this country only fifty years ago. What happens when all the birds are gone?'

There was a tense silence in the room, broken by the Duchess. She put a hand on my arm and turned to Etta. 'Etta dear, there is no need to pounce on poor Henrietta. Let us not judge her.

Let her hear what we have to say.'

And so I sat and listened. The ladies discussed how they wanted to join their groups together to stop women wearing feathers for fashion.

'It is in the best interests to be based in London,' declared Etta Smith. 'We have the use of the offices here.'

The Duchess of Portland agreed. 'But I think we keep the name, the Society for the Protection of Birds. And who knows, maybe one day we will be able to have royal approval.'

The doctor poured another cup of tea for everyone and held up her teacup. 'To the Society for the Protection of Birds,' she cheered. 'The SPB.'

We raised our teacups too. 'To the SPB.'

It was funny really, sitting in that room, with dust motes dancing in the shafts of sunlight that sliced through the darkness. I had a strange feeling that I was witnessing the beginning of something extraordinary, like the first shoot that emerges from an acorn to anchor roots into the ground for a mighty oak.

'Excellent,' said Etta. 'Together we can raise

our voices and tell other women to care for wild creatures and not have them killed for decoration.'

Kitty nodded. 'And this is exactly the reason women should have the vote. We need our voices to be heard.'

Teacups clinked on saucers in the silence that followed.

The Duchess smiled at Kitty. 'You know we don't all agree with you, Kitty. Many of us here today do not support women having the vote. Let us save that argument for another day.'

Aunt Katherine's brow looked furrowed but she did not speak.

When we climbed back into the carriage to return home, Aunt Katherine turned to me and pulled a small, wrapped present from her bag. 'I almost forgot. A little birthday gift.'

'Thank you,' I said. I opened it to find a pretty enamelled hand mirror.

'You must call me Kitty,' said Aunt Katherine. 'Aunt Katherine is such a stuffy name. Besides, I am nearer to your age than your father's. And I shan't call you Henrietta. I'll let your mother do that.' She smiled. 'From now on, I shall call you Hen.'

I stared at my reflection in the mirror on the way home. My mind was a whirl. Murdered birds, women doctors, and women's votes? My reflection stared back, and for the first time I felt I didn't really know the girl in front of me.

'Well, Hen?' said Kitty as the cab pulled up outside our house. 'What do you think of the new Society for the Protection of Birds?'

'I can't see what harm it can do to try to help the birds,' I said.

Kitty laughed at this, then said something that stayed with me: 'This isn't just a meeting of a group of delicate society ladies. This isn't just about birds, Hen. This is about women. It's about freedom and fighting men's rule. These are dangerous meetings. They have the power to change the world.'

Mother and Father both came to say goodnight to me in the nursery. I think they wanted to know about my meeting with the Duchess of Portland. I told them how delightful and charming I found her.

Then I felt a bit daring. I asked Father if women could be doctors.

Father tucked me in bed. 'I have heard of women doctors, but I believe they are quite peculiar folk.'

'It's not natural,' said Mother. 'Besides, being a surgeon demands nerves of steel. I shouldn't want a lady doctor fainting at the first sight of blood.'

I ventured further, only to regret it. 'Do you think women should be allowed to vote?'

Father laughed at this. 'Next you'll be asking me if a woman could be the Prime Minister.'

Mother was not so amused. 'What has Aunt Katherine being saying?'

'Nothing,' I said. 'Nothing at all. I was just thinking, that's all.'

'Well don't!' Mother snapped so sharply that I heard Lettie whimper in her sleep. 'Too much thinking is a dangerous thing.'

So here you find me, dear friend, sitting in bed and unable to sleep, my mind racing with the most wild and dangerous thoughts.

CHAPTER 8

Semira heard Mama and Robel return. She could hear their voices in the kitchen below. But she didn't want to go downstairs. She sat thinking about Hen, and dangerous thoughts swirled into Semira's head too. Why did Robel think he could tell them what to do? What if she challenged Robel? What would he do to her? What would he do to Mama?

The smell of frying onions and spices drifted up the stairs. Semira tucked the diary back into her drawer and went down to the kitchen.

Mama was stirring chopped onions for a chicken stew and Robel was sitting at the table working on his computer. He never let Semira use the computer, not even for homework.

Mama looked up. 'How was school?'

'Fine,' said Semira. Her stomach growled with hunger but she didn't want to ask for some food in front of Robel.

'Robel has some good news,' said Mama. 'He met with the immigration officer today. Now that we have had refugee status for five years, he thinks we may be allowed to settle here permanently.'

'When will we know?' said Semira.

Mama shrugged her shoulders. 'We have to have more checks, more questions. I don't have any documents. They want proof of marriage too.'

'But you're not married to Robel,' scowled Semira.

Robel glared at her over the top of his computer. 'This isn't a game, Semira! Don't let me hear you say that again.'

Semira leaned against the worktop and watched Mama stirring the onions. She tried to read Mama's expression but her face was a blank mask and impossible to know. Is this what Mama wanted, for Robel to live with them for ever and tell them what to do?

'Hey, Semira,' ordered Robel, still typing. 'Pass me a Coke from the fridge.'

Semira looked past Mama, to Robel and the big fridge-freezer standing between them. What would happen if she challenged him? 'You're closer.'

Robel stopped what he was doing and stared at her. 'What did you just say?'

Semira felt her heart thump inside her chest, but she folded her arms and stared back. 'I said you're closer to the fridge. You can reach it yourself.'

'Get me a Coke, Semira,' ordered Robel.

Semira didn't move.

Robel slammed the laptop shut. 'Don't forget who earns the money here,' he said, pointing his finger at her.

Semira glanced at Mama, but Mama opened the fridge and handed the Coke to Semira. 'Give Robel his drink, Semira.'

Semira's hands were trembling. She felt

angry with Robel and even angrier with Mama for not standing up for her. She thumped the drink down next to Robel.

'Good,' snapped Robel. He grabbed the drink. 'I'm going to watch TV.' He stood up to leave but stopped to face Semira. 'Remember. You are my daughter now. Don't forget that.' He held his finger in her face, 'You are here to serve *me*.'

Semira watched him go then turned to Mama. 'Why do you let him treat us like this?'

Mama began cutting up pieces of chicken. 'Semira, this is our chance of staying here. We can't go back.'

'But why Robel? Why can't it be you and me?'

Mama paused. 'Because we need him. Because if anyone finds out we have lied to immigration, we all go back.'

'I hate him,' said Semira. 'I'd rather go back.'

'Semira!' Mama brought the knife down on the meat. 'You have no idea what we left. No idea. You were too young.'

'I'm going upstairs,' said Semira. She left the

room and slammed the door after her.

Semira heard Mama's footsteps on the stairs, and checked the diary was hidden away. She didn't want to share it with Mama somehow. It was private. Maybe if she told her mother, it would spoil the magic. Maybe Hen wouldn't seem so real. Semira pulled her maths book from her bag to make it look like she was about to do some homework.

Her mother slipped into the room with a bowl of chicken stew for each of them. The spices made Semira's mouth water. Mama closed the door and locked it and sat on the end of the bed. This is how they liked to eat, away from the kitchen and other people in the house, in peace.

'Semira, don't be cross with me about Robel,' said Mama. 'I am trying to do what is best for us.'

'I'm sorry, Mama.'

'I still have you, and that is the most important thing of all,' said Mama. 'Maybe one day we will have a flat with a garden or balcony to sit out in the sunshine.'

Semira ate slowly, savouring the taste. Mama had piled extra rice for Semira and by the time she had finished she was feeling full for the first time in a long while. She placed her finished bowl to the side and opened her maths book.

Mama peered over. 'Do you want some help?'

Semira smiled. Mama was a natural at maths. It came as easily to her as breathing. 'Yes please. Everyone knew what they were doing. I didn't have time to ask the teacher.'

Mama finished her stew, wiping the bowl with bread, then rubbed her hands. Semira noticed a sparkle come into her eye. This was something Mama could do, and she could do it well.

Semira wrapped the duvet around her while Mama looked at the questions. She was a good teacher, slow and patient. By the end of the homework, Semira could understand the maths. She put her book aside and climbed into her nightclothes and curled back beneath the duvet. There was a damp chill in the air. The room they shared was on the north side of the house and black mildew stained the corner walls.

'Mama, why can't we go back to Eritrea?' said Semira. 'Is it so bad?'

Mama sighed. She never spoke of her past. 'It's complicated,' she said. 'There was so much hope when Eritrea won independence. My parents died fighting for our freedom and I was sent to relatives who owned a farm. But the women who had fought for the country didn't get the equality they wanted. Things turned bad. People were put in prison for speaking out about the government. Then there was a terrible drought. There was no money or food. When our crops failed for the third time, we moved to the city. My cousins were taken into military service.' Mama stood up to walk over to the window and stared out into the evening. 'I was twenty at the time. I never saw them again.'

'What happened to you then?' asked Semira.

'Hush Semira. I'll take these bowls to wash

while you get some sleep. I have to work again tonight, so I won't be back until after midnight.'

Semira tried to get to sleep but it was too early. She could hear the TV blaring from the room downstairs, but she didn't feel comfortable going down and being amongst the men.

She lay in bed staring at the bird on the hat and thinking about the green bird in her memory. Patrick had said it could never be caged.

Thoughts of birds and freedom swirled around in her head. She wondered what Hen was doing. How strange it seemed that she and Hen were parted by over a hundred years, and yet it felt as if their lives were somehow so close, as if two floating bubbles pressed against each other, touching, yet separate.

Semira pulled the diary from the drawer, opened the pages, and looked through into Hen's world.

CHAPTER 9

Friday 15th May, 1891

Dear Friend,

What an extraordinary day!

I have never before been betwixt the fear of
death and utter joy as I have today, but I would
do it all over again if I could.

It is quite hard to know where to begin, but
I will begin with the doorbell ringing just after
breakfast and Mrs Tindall announcing that
Aunt Katherine had arrived to ask for my
assistance for an errand in Town.

Mother was in bed complaining of suffering
from her nerves and Father agreed to let me go,

only because Mrs Tindall said that I would get under her feet all day. She said she had some important baking to do for one of Mother's tea parties. Mrs Tindall always does the baking because Cook has hot hands and ruins the pastry.

Kitty told me that we would be taking air on Primrose Hill and to make sure I wore stout boots and warm bloomers beneath my dress.

When she said we would be taking tea with her doctor friend, Georgina Lewis, she flashed me such a wicked smile that it made me think the day would involve more than just refreshment and a brisk walk.

'How should I address the doctor?' I asked. 'Should I say Dr Lewis?'

Kitty laughed. 'She cannot bear such stuffiness. She likes her friends to call her Georgie.'

The doctor's house is quite different from any I have seen. Inside it is so light and bright, without any of the heavy furnishings of our house. There are paintings on the walls too. Not the hunting scenes in dark oil colours that Father seems to like, but paintings with bright colours that have no shape or form at all.

Chapter 9

The doctor saw me looking at them.

'What do they make you feel?' she said.

'Feel?'

The doctor smiled. 'These paintings ask questions of you.'

I sat down with a glass of lemonade and stared at a painting, not quite sure what to say. I fear my awkwardness drove me to embarrass myself.

I asked if her husband, Mr Lewis, collected other paintings. The doctor said that there was no Mr Lewis and seemed amused at my question.

'Georgie doesn't need a husband,' said Kitty. 'She is a woman of profession and property. She can afford the luxury of not having a man.'

Georgie laughed at this and said she would happily get married if the right man were to come along, but they appeared to be few and far between. 'Men are afraid of intelligent women,' she said.

'But surely,' Kitty said, 'You have met many suitable educated men.'

Georgie sighed. 'Some of the most educated men I have met are the dullest of them all. Intelligence isn't measured by your education,' she said. 'It is measured by your curiosity about the world.'

'I for one shall never get married,' declared Kitty. 'I will not be a man's possession, breeding cow, or trophy for him to wear upon his arm. I will answer only to myself.'

Georgie sipped her tea. 'Enough talk of marriage for today. It is time to do what you came here for.' She opened a box full of addressed envelopes. 'These are letters to various dignitaries asking for their support for the SPB.'

She showed us one letter and it listed the number of birds sold in London on one day alone last year: 8,000 parrots, 2,000 woodpeckers, 30,000 hummingbirds, 4,000 kingfishers, several hundred owls and hawks and 800,000 pairs of wings . . . to name some of the many types of birds for sale.

Georgie put the letters into two canvas bags. 'You can ride with one each and hand-deliver them,' she said.

I explained that I had ridden a horse only once before at a farm near Bath. Mother always said horse riding was far too dangerous for girls.

She laughed and said that the horses we would

65

be riding have two wheels, not four legs. 'I have two of the new safety bicycles.'

I protested that I had never ridden a bicycle.

Kitty put her hands on her hips. 'Then, Miss Henrietta, you will have to learn too.'

I followed Kitty and Georgie outside and around the back of the house to a small backstreet. Georgie unlocked the door of one of the stables and showed us two safety bicycles. I had never seen one close up before. They are very different to the penny-farthing bicycle that Father once tried to ride. The penny-farthing has one huge wheel and one small wheel and the rider sits high above the ground. The safety bicycle has two wheels that are the same size. These ones have the new air tyres too, not the solid rubber ones. The rider sits on the saddle, so that both feet can touch the ground. Yet, I could not understand how one could balance on such a thing.

'Right,' said Georgie. 'Let's get started.'

I must say, she made it look so easy, the way she lifted her skirt and stepped one foot over the frame of the bicycle. She lifted the pedal with her foot and pushed off, pedalling sedately up and down the road. 'The trick is,' she called to us, 'to keep moving. The faster you go, the easier it becomes.'

She stopped and stepped off the bicycle. 'Kitty, my dear, you try first.'

Kitty put her leg over the frame and gripped the handlebars. 'Ugh, my skirts get in the way.'

'You'll get used to it,' said Georgie. She held the saddle while Kitty pushed on the pedals and she was off, faster and faster until Georgie had to let go. She seemed perfectly balanced until I saw her skirts become tangled in the wheel spokes and she and the bicycle came crashing down with such force that I feared she and the bicycle were broken beyond repair.

I was most concerned for Kitty's welfare, but Georgie had to hold her sides from laughing so much. Kitty did not share her amusement. She stood up, and to my shock, pulled off her skirt to reveal a pair of men's breeches, held by a belt. Her bare calves showed between her knees and ankles.

'If women are to cycle,' she said, 'then they will have to change their clothes to be of more practical use.'

Georgie seemed to think it amusing. 'It is most unladylike,' she laughed. 'I suggest you give up immediately.'

Kitty looked most vexed. 'I don't give a fig for your suggestion. I want to learn how to cycle.'

She tried again, and this time she got up some speed, bumping over the cobbles until she stopped at the end of the road and crashed to the side.

'You're supposed to put your feet down,' called Georgie.

Kitty set off again and cycled towards us, a big grin on her face. 'You simply must try, Hen dear. It is most invigorating.'

'Yes,' agreed Georgie. 'Would you like to?'

I looked around and could not see another soul in sight. There was something about it that made me want to try. I took the handlebars and stepped my foot over the frame. It was quite peculiar, really. It somehow felt natural folding my hands around the handlebars. I pulled my skirt a little way up, aware my bloomers were showing beneath the hem. It is a good thing my skirt is a little short as I am sure that is why it did not become tangled in the wheels.

Kitty held the saddle as I pedalled. 'Faster!' I could hear Georgie calling. 'It becomes easier the faster you go.'

And so I pedalled faster and faster and found myself travelling at quite a speed.

When I came to the end of the road I stuck my two feet out to come to a stop. I turned the bicycle around and pushed down hard on the pedal. It wobbled but I found myself flying along again, the wind in my face.

Kitty clapped hard. 'Oh well done, Hen, you're a natural. You haven't even fallen off.'

Georgie helped us with the canvas bags and sent us out to post the letters through the letterboxes of some rather grand houses. Kitty refused to wear her skirt and rode in her breeches and riding jacket, head high, ignoring the stares from men and women taking air in the park.

When we had completed our task, we pushed the bicycles to the top of Primrose Hill and looked down at London spread out before us. There was a fresh breeze that cooled our flushed cheeks.

'We're changing the world doing this, Hen,' said Kitty. 'We are saving the birds. One day, people won't wear feathers for fashion and they won't even know it was the two of us who put the first letters through people's doors. But we will know. You and me. We will always know.'

'You and me,' I said. And I felt such a rush of affection for Kitty. Her free spirit can make anything seem possible.

Kitty grinned widely and swung her leg over the bicycle. 'You and me, for ever.'

I turned my face up to the sun. 'For ever,' I shouted.

'Race you,' said Kitty.

She set off and I followed close behind. The slope of the hill gave us such momentum to keep going, that I could swear my wheels hardly touched the ground.

I don't think I have ever felt my heart pounding as fast as it did on our descent. The grass was a blur beside me. It was a moment of utter fear and joy combined. I have never felt as alive as I did then. I was so taken by it that I did not care what anyone thought of me. It was just Kitty and me and the bicycles and the wind rushing past. It was the closest thing to flying.

'Woohooooo!' called Kitty. 'Wooooohoooooooooooo!'

I came to a stop beside Kitty at the bottom of the hill and caught my breath. I think my smile was as big as hers. I looked back at the top of the hill and all I could think is that I wished to do it all over again.

I was still flushed with excitement, when a man came up to us and rapped his cane on Kitty's bicycle.

'You are a disgrace,' he shouted. He was so vexed that spittle formed at his mouth and caught in his moustache. I was quite fearful that he might want to hit Kitty. I was too struck dumb to say anything, but Kitty looked him coolly in the eye and told him to remove his cane from the bicycle or she would be sending him the damage costs.

When we returned the bicycles, Georgie laughed at Kitty's story and said we could borrow the bicycles any time we wanted.

We were late home and in such a hurry that Kitty climbed in the cab and forgot to collect her skirt. She walked me into the house in just the men's pair of breeches and her riding jacket.

Father was home at the time. He looked Kitty up and down and fixed his gaze upon her bare legs. 'Kitty! What is the meaning of this vulgarity?'

Kitty rolled her eyes. 'Oh brother dearest, these are only legs. I'm sure you've seen them before. Why, I do believe you have a pair of your own.'

Father looked quite angered. 'I hope you have not been out in public like this. In the eyes of God you have been shamefully immodest. Men will stare.'

Kitty looked equally angered. She put her hands on her hips. 'In the eyes of God, dear brother, it is for men to look away, not for me to cover up with clothes. Maybe if they can't keep their hands or eyes to themselves, it is they who are shameful. Like Uncle Gerald,' she added.

Father raised his voice. 'Kitty! Do not speak ill of the dead.'

'I never spoke well of him in life,' said Kitty. 'God bless Uncle Gerald. May he rot in hell.'

Father and Kitty just glared at each other in silence until Mrs Tindall came into the room with a tray of tea and cake.

Father turned to me before he stormed out of the room. 'Take the tray up for your mother, Henrietta, and do not mention this incident. I fear it will not be good for her nerves.'

When we were alone again, Kitty turned to me. 'Hen dear, I did so enjoy the day with you. It was the most marvellous fun. I hope we can do it again. You and me.'

I couldn't help a huge smile spreading on my face too. 'You and me, for ever.'

'Oh Hen, bicycles are going to change the world for women.'

'You really think so?' I said.

'I know so,' said Kitty. 'We shan't wear these ridiculous big skirts for long. I dare say that soon we shall be wearing breeches like men. We will be free. We could go anywhere we wished. Why, we could travel the world on a bicycle.'

'Oh Kitty, you are funny,' I said.

'I'm being serious, Hen. Why, tomorrow I shall borrow one of the doctor's bicycles and cycle to the seaside at Brighton.'

I laughed at that.

'I will,' said Kitty.

'It would be awfully dangerous for a woman all on her own. I don't think you would get far before a man might stop you.'

'I shall do it, Hen,' said Kitty. 'I shall bring you back some pebbles from the beach.'

'It's a long way, at least fifty miles,' I said.

She looked at me. 'I shall do it tomorrow. I shall come by here and wave before I go.'

I am now writing from the nursery. Lettie wanted a story before bed, and so I made one up about a girl who could ride a magical bicycle that could soar above the rooftops anywhere in the world. Lettie said she was a little afraid of riding a flying bicycle and so I said we could ride in her magical bed. We flew across oceans and deserts before coming back into our bedroom. Lettie's eyes were shining with the excitement of it. I wondered too, if it were possible to travel anywhere in the world and see these places.

I am going to bed now although I can't help wonder if Kitty will pass by tomorrow morning on her way to Brighton.

I dare say I shall not sleep at all.

Saturday 16th May, 1891

Dearest Friend,

This is a short entry, being written before breakfast, but I simply must tell you what has happened. I woke to the sound of small stones hitting my window. I looked down to see some insolent boy on a bicycle throwing stones at me. Just when I was about to close the window again, the young boy doffed his cap and waved it at me. There was something about his appearance that was familiar, and then I realized it was my dear Kitty with her hair tied up. She was wearing a tweed jacket, breeches, and a flat cap.

'I'm off to Brighton,' she called up to me. 'Wish me luck. I took your advice and did not want to be stopped by some enraged man who was scared of a woman, so I have dressed as a boy.'

'Brighton is so far away,' I called down.

'I shall stay there with a friend tonight and return tomorrow,' called Kitty.

'Aren't you afraid?' I asked.

'I'm not afraid of anything,' Kitty called back.

With that she was gone, pedalling away down the street.

I watched her go. I watched long after she had turned the corner and disappeared between the cabs.

She is fearless.

Utterly fearless.

And as I sit here in my room, how I wish that one day I could be as brave as she is too.

CHAPTER 10

Where there isn't any food to eat, suddenly food seems to be everywhere.

Semira's stomach rumbled, but there was nothing for breakfast. Robel had hidden all the food in revenge for Semira's outburst the night before. She wished she hadn't said anything and just handed Robel the drink. It hadn't fixed anything and it now meant she and Mama went hungry.

Semira walked to school, aching with hunger. The scent of coffee and pastries hung in the air. She walked past vegetable stalls, sweet with smell of mango and melon. She even wondered if she could help herself to a leftover bagel on a coffee shop table.

She sat through morning classes trying to concentrate on maths and trying to ignore the groaning pit in her stomach.

'You coming to lunch?' said Holly.

Semira shook her head. 'I'm not feeling great,' she said. She wondered how many more excuses she could make to avoid going to lunch.

Chloe frowned. 'Do you want to go to the sick room?'

'I'm OK,' said Semira. 'Something didn't agree with me last night.'

At lunchtime she stayed in the library and borrowed some books to read for the long evenings alone without Mama. Patrick was in the library, eating sandwiches surreptitiously at another table. Maybe he avoided lunchtimes too. Semira felt light-headed and rested her head in her arms on the table. Her mind kept turning back to Kitty. Did she make it to Brighton? She was still thinking about her at the end of school when she joined the mass of pupils surging out through the school gates.

Ahead of her she saw Patrick. He was alone

again, his head down, hands deep in pockets. Two boys joined him, flanking either side of him. They looked much older than him, and bigger too. At first Semira thought they were being friendly, but then, in one swift movement, one boy pushed his shoulder into Patrick, pinning him against the school fence. The other tipped Patrick's rucksack upside down, spilling the contents. Patrick handed something from his pocket to one of the boys and they walked on, as if nothing had happened. It was all over in seconds. Patrick scooped his books back in his bag, straightened his blazer, and joined the crowd.

Semira stopped and stared, unable to move. Patrick had been bullied in broad daylight. No one had stopped to help. It seemed no one had even noticed. Yet, other pupils had taken a wide berth around him. It was as if he was invisible, as if nothing unusual had happened at all.

'You OK?'

Semira spun around to see Holly and Chloe behind her.

'Two boys just set on Patrick,' said Semira.

Holly glanced at Chloe. 'That'll be Mad Dog and his mates.'

'You don't want to mess with them,' said Chloe.

'Shouldn't we say something?' said Semira.

'Only if you want them to pick on you next too,' said Holly.

'They'll leave him alone soon and pick on someone else,' said Chloe. 'My cousin changed primary school because of them.'

'It's not right,' said Semira.

'It's what they do,' said Holly. 'Everyone knows it.'

Semira just stared at the space where Patrick had been.

'We're going to get ice cream in the park on the way home,' said Holly. 'D'you want to come?'

Semira shook her head. 'I've got to get back.' She watched them cross the road and then she walked on past the spot where the boys had pushed Patrick up against the fence. A book lay in the dirt, its cover trampled and torn.

She picked it up and turned the pages. It was a notebook, full of pictures and lists of different birds. The birds had ticked boxes next to them and there were lots of scribbled notes. It was almost like a diary, she thought. A bird diary. She looked up again to see if she could see Patrick further down the road, but he was nowhere in sight. She flipped through the book again and on the first page was Patrick's name and address.

She slipped the book in her bag. Would Patrick want his book today? Maybe she should wait for tomorrow and give it to him in class, but then she'd have to explain in front of everyone how she came to have it. She stopped a postman emptying a letter box to ask for directions to the address inside the book.

The postman pushed the letters into his sack. 'Down the high street, turn left before the park and it's the first estate on the left.'

It was on her way home so Semira could drop it off. She reached the address and stood outside a semi-detached house, its front garden laid to gravel. Semira reached up and rang the front doorbell. As she waited, she couldn't help glance inside the open garage. Bicycles filled the space from floor to ceiling. There were bicycles with chunky tyres and wide handlebars, bicycles with thin smooth tyres and dropped handlebars. Some had wheels and some were hanging wheel-less from the ceiling. There were boxes with saddles and other boxes with bicycle chains and toothed cogs of different sizes. A man answered the door wearing shorts and a T-shirt, and he was rubbing his hands in a cloth stained black with oil.

'Is Patrick in?' asked Semira.

The man smiled. 'Who shall I say it is?'

'Semira, a school friend,' she said.

The man held the door open. 'I'm Graham. Come on in, and I'll call Patrick.'

Semira followed him through to the kitchen. A bright-yellow bike lay upside down on the table, resting on the handlebars and saddle.

'Patrick!' yelled Graham. 'Someone here to see you.'

Patrick came down the stairs, and just stared at Semira.

'I brought your book back,' she said, holding it out.

Patrick glanced at Graham and then at the book. 'Thanks,' he said, taking it from her. He flicked though the pages. 'I must've dropped it.'

Semira watched him. Clearly he hadn't told Graham about the bullying.

Graham washed his hands under the tap. 'You'll stay for a slice of cake will you Semira? I made it earlier. Victoria sponge with strawberry jam and cream.'

Semira looked at the large cake dusted with icing sugar and again her stomach rumbled. She hadn't eaten all day. 'Yes please, if that's OK.'

'I'll just put my tools away,' said Graham. 'Patrick, can you put the kettle on and get some plates out?'

'I'm sorry about your book,' said Semira once Graham had left the room.

'It's OK,' said Patrick.

'Have you reported those boys?'

Patrick shook his head. 'Don't say anything.

I don't want Graham or Mum to know. They'd only worry.'

'You can't just let them get away with it,' said Semira.

'It's fine. Really. I don't get hurt,' said Patrick. 'I just give Mad Dog a couple of quid.'

Semira watched Patrick put the plates on the table and cut the cake. 'I'm sorry I ran off yesterday. I was upset, that's all.'

'S'OK,' said Patrick. 'I'm always putting my big foot in it somehow.'

Graham came back into the kitchen and lifted the bike down from the table. 'Well that one's done.'

Semira turned her attention back to the bike. She thought about Kitty cycling all the way to Brighton. 'Was it broken?'

Patrick put a huge slice of cake on each plate. 'Graham buys up old bits of junk and tries to turn them into bicycles.'

Graham wagged his finger at her. 'Don't listen to him, Semira. I find old bicycles people don't want any more and do them up. I call it re-cycling.'

Patrick groaned at the joke he had heard Graham say a thousand times before.

'Well, it's good for the planet and it makes me a bit of money too,' said Graham. He poured boiling water into the teapot. 'Besides, Patrick and Lily like joining me on my rides.'

A girl who looked older than Patrick walked into the kitchen and helped herself to a huge slice of cake. 'Dad's not going on about bikes again, is he?'

Patrick rolled his eyes. 'Mum says it's a midlife crisis.'

Graham laughed. 'Well there are worse things than bicycles and cycling Lycra when you get to my age.'

Lily turned to Semira. 'Dad's so old his first bike was a penny-farthing.'

'Not even I'm that old,' said Graham.

'Watch out,' said Patrick, 'He'll try to sell you a bike next.'

Graham turned to Semira. 'Do you like cycling?'

Semira shrugged her shoulders. 'I've never tried.'

Patrick's hand stopped mid-air, about to stuff a piece of cake into his mouth. 'What, never?'

Semira shook her head. How could she explain about her life, how they were always on the move, without money or anything to their name.'

'It's the best thing,' said Graham. 'You should try.'

'We could teach you,' said Patrick.

'Only if you want to,' said Graham. 'It's hard getting started.'

Patrick offered Semira another slice of cake. 'Do you want to have a go?'

Semira thought of Hen and Kitty.

Maybe if she hadn't read the diary, she would have passed up the opportunity but there was something about the thought of it. She wanted to join Hen and Kitty on their bicycles. She wanted to feel the freedom of it.

'Yes please,' Semira grinned. 'I'd love to.'

CHAPTER 11

'You'll have to borrow a helmet,' said Graham. 'You can try out this bike I've been working on.'

'I'll take my bike too,' said Patrick. 'We'll go to the park and try there.'

It wasn't far walking the bikes to the park, and when Semira saw the long paths through the grass, she began to feel more and more nervous.

'I'll hold you,' said Patrick.

Semira stepped over the frame and held onto the handlebars. She had the strange feeling she had done this before. Maybe it was reading the diary. Maybe she felt she had been cycling with Hen already. She tried to remember what the doctor had said. *Go faster. It's easier the faster you go.*

Be brave, thought Semira. Be brave, like Hen. Be brave like Kitty.

Patrick held onto Semira's coat at first. The bicycle felt wobbly, but as Semira picked up speed down the hill, Patrick let go and she was cycling all by herself. She could hear Patrick's feet running on the ground behind her, but even he seemed far behind as the wind rushed past her face. She pushed her feet on the pedals, going faster and faster, *like flying*, she thought.

'Brake, Semira, BRAKE!' Patrick shouted.

Semira could see a busy road ahead rushing towards her. If she didn't stop she'd fly straight into the traffic. She pulled on the brakes and the next thing she knew she was spiralling through the air; sky and ground whirling around her, until she and the bike bounced and landed on the grass.

Patrick rushed up. 'Are you OK?'

Semira rubbed her back. 'Think so. What happened?'

'I forgot to say to pull on the brakes slowly,' said Patrick. 'You flipped right over.'

Semira got to her feet and picked the bike from the ground. 'I hope it's not broken.'

Patrick checked it over. 'It's fine.' He looked up at Semira. 'Probably best you get home in one piece. Shall we go back?'

'I'd like another go,' said Semira. 'Can I?'

Patrick helped Semira onto the bike again. This time she pulled on the brakes slowly and began to manage the steering and corners.

'You're getting the hang of it,' he said.

Semira grinned.

'We could go on for a bit,' said Patrick. 'There's a lake I cycle around. It's a bird reserve too.'

'Cool,' said Semira. She pushed off and followed behind him, watching the ground blur beneath her. It was strangely hypnotic, her feet pushing the pedals, the whirr of the wheels and the flow of the bike.

Patrick pulled up at the side of a path and Semira slammed on the brakes, almost bumping into him.

'You could've said you were stopping,' said Semira.

'Sorry,' said Patrick. 'I thought we'd stop here. I usually do.'

He pulled a bike lock from his rucksack and locked the bikes to the fence. Semira read the sign: *Heron Hide. Royal Society for the Protection of Birds (RSPB) reserve.*

She followed him along a wooden walkway into the reeds at the end of the lake, where the walkway stopped at a wooden hut.

Patrick turned to her. 'We have to be quiet,' he whispered.

There was no one else inside the bird hide. Patrick scanned the noticeboard to see if any unusual birds had visited that day, and then sat on the bench by the window. 'I should have brought my binoculars.'

Semira put her arms on the window ledge and stared out. All was still except for a bird with black feathers and a white beak moving jerkily across the water.

'Coot,' said Patrick. 'There are tons of coots and moorhens here.'

Semira looked across at him. 'Is this being a twitcher?'

'Sort of,' said Patrick.

'Do you just sit and watch the birds?' asked Semira.

Patrick was silent for a while. 'It's not just for the birds,' he said. 'It's quiet here too. No one bothers you here.'

Semira stared out over the water.

'See that post there,' said Patrick. 'The one by that tree stump.'

Semira kept her eyes on the post, and blinked as a flash of electric blue came to rest upon it.

'Kingfisher,' whispered Patrick. 'He always comes here at this time of day.'

'It's odd to think thousands of them were killed for hats years ago,' said Semira.

Patrick turned to look at her. 'What makes you say that?'

Semira shrugged her shoulders. It couldn't hurt to tell Patrick about the diary. 'I found a Victorian diary at the market. It lists birds killed for their feathers. It came with a hat with a stuffed Abyssinian Lovebird. That's what I was looking up on the computer the other day.'

'Cool,' said Patrick. 'I wish I'd found it. I've got a fox skull and a crow's wing at home.'

'Ugh that's gross,' said Semira.

'No more gross than wanting a dead bird on a hat,' said Patrick. 'In fact that's just plain weird.'

'I guess so,' said Semira. 'In the diary it says there were women who started a group called the Society for the Protection of Birds. You don't think it's the same charity as the RSPB that runs this reserve do you?'

'I'll look it up,' said Patrick. He tapped on his phone. 'Can you remember their names?'

Semira frowned. 'There was an Etta someone and a Duchess of Portland . . . '

Patrick's eyebrows shot up. 'You're kidding? These are real people. It says it here. The Duchess of Portland managed to get royal approval. It became the RSPB in 1904.'

'No way,' said Semira. She stared out over the lake. It was turning gold in the early evening sunshine. A breeze bent the reeds and rippled the surface of the water, and a flock of small birds swept up into the air, and swirled and flurried before disappearing in the reeds again.

The kingfisher dived, scattering diamond drops of water. It flew to its perch with a small fish in its beak. Semira thought about Kitty and Hen cycling to hand out letters for the Society for the Protection of Birds and how places like this might not be here if it weren't for those women at the very beginning.

'You wouldn't think we were in the city,' said Semira. 'It's like a different world.'

'It's why I like it,' said Patrick. 'When we lived with Dad, I came here to get away from home. I'd stay all day. It's my escape from school too. I can put up with Mad Dog because I know this place is here.'

CHAPTER 12

Semira ran home from Patrick's house. She hadn't realized how late it had become. She hoped Mama and Robel would be out, but they were both in the kitchen.

Mama stood up. 'Semira, is that you?'

'Yes Mama.'

'Where have you been?' she said, 'I was so worried. I didn't know what to do.'

'I'm sorry, Mama,'

'Why were you late?' asked Robel.

'I was at a friend's house,' said Semira.

'Who is this friend?' demanded Robel.

'Patrick,' said Semira.

'A boy?' said Robel. 'You shouldn't be going home with boys. What were you doing?'

'Homework,' said Semira.

'Liar,' snapped Robel. 'What were you doing?'

Semira glared back at him. 'I was using a computer.'

'And what else,' said Robel. 'What else were you doing?'

'If you really want to know,' said Semira, 'I was learning how to ride a bike.'

She wasn't prepared for Robel's reaction. His jaw hung open and he just stared at her. Then he spun round to face Mama. 'What have you been telling her?'

'Nothing,' said Mama.

Robel grabbed Mama roughly by the arms. 'What have you said to her?'

'Get off her,' Semira shouted. 'Leave her alone.'

Robel stepped back. 'You don't deserve me,' he spat. 'Either of you.'

'Come, child,' Mama whispered, ushering Semira upstairs. 'Don't upset Robel.' She sat with Semira on the bed. 'I have to go out to work tonight. Stay here and don't go out, promise?'

'I promise, Mama.'

'Good.'

'Mama?'

'Yes?'

'Why was Robel so angry about me riding a bike?'

'Leave it, Semira. Enough talk for tonight.'

'It was only a bike.'

'Enough, Semira,' snapped Mama.

'Why are you angry too? What is it about a bike?'

'Semira! Enough.'

'Mama!'

'Semira! I don't ever want to hear you have been riding a bicycle again.'

Semira glared at her mother, the silence thick between them. Mama got up to leave and Semira didn't even say goodbye. She waited until Mama had left the room, then slammed the door behind her and locked it.

She felt trapped inside a room full of secrets. Trapped with nowhere to go.

What would Hen do?

What would Kitty do?

Semira opened the diary and began to read.

Wednesday 20th May, 1891

Dearest Friend,

Four days have passed since Kitty left for Brighton and until this morning there had been no word from her. I was almost beside myself with worry. Mrs Tindall told me to stop pacing in the parlour because I would wear away the floorboards, though I did notice her peering out of the window quite often too.

And so it was a great relief when Mrs Tindall announced the arrival of Kitty just after breakfast today.

Mother was out of bed and sitting in the garden room in the early-morning sunshine.

'Good day, Katherine,' Mother said.

I notice now how Mother can barely let herself look at Kitty.

'Good day to you, Josephine,' said Kitty. 'I wonder if Miss Henrietta might like to join me and pay a visit to my dear friend the Duchess of

Portland. She says she has a favour to ask of us.'

Mother sipped her tea.

'I should like that, Mother,' I said.

'I'm not sure she should go,' said Mother. 'Henrietta has seemed a little tired recently.'

'Oh, such a shame,' said Kitty. 'The Duchess seems quite taken with Henrietta and had mentioned about sending an invitation to you all to her garden party in the summer.'

Even I could see the vexation in Mother's face. 'Of course, Katherine. I am delighted to know that the Duchess can see we have such a gracious daughter. It reflects well upon our family.'

'Cake?' said Mrs Tindall.

I hadn't noticed her enter the room with a plate of sponge slices.

'Orange blossom and honey,' she said, 'with a secret vanilla cream filling.'

Mother frowned. 'Mrs Tindall! It is only just past breakfast. Do you think we have taken leave of our senses? Do you think we are as gluttonous as pigs at a trough?'

Kitty smiled. 'It looks wonderful cake, Mrs Tindall. Though I too am a little replete after breakfast myself, but I should be keen to try some later if you have a little to spare.'

Mrs Tindall smiled. 'I shall put a slice in a box for you to take with you, Miss Katherine.'

Once again, I noticed something in the air shift a little. Mrs Tindall's smile seemed laden with secrets, just like the cream inside her cake.

Kitty turned to me and winked. 'It is a little fresh today for crossing the park. I suggest stout boots and thick bloomers.'

'Yes, Aunt Katherine,' I said. I curtsied to Mother and Kitty, but inside, my heart was pounding with excitement. I couldn't wait, for I knew that today we would be riding bicycles again.

Kitty and I set off across the park to the doctor's house.

'We shall meet the Duchess of Portland there,' said Kitty. 'She has a favour to ask of us.'

Kitty had set a fast pace and I trotted to keep up with her. I was bursting to ask her about her trip to Brighton.

I think she must have guessed what was on

my mind for she turned to me and gave such a smile that it seemed to match the sunshine of the morning. 'Oh Hen, I expect you wish to see pebbles from Brighton beach?'

I nodded. 'Oh Kitty, did you make it there? Tell me you did.'

Kitty shook her head. 'I never made it.'

I must have looked most glum because Kitty stopped and took both my hands in hers. 'Oh Hen, don't feel troubled. You see, the most remarkable thing has happened and I have been almost dying with excitement to share it with you.'

'What is it?' I said.

'Oh Hen, my dearest. It is the most wonderful thing.'

'What?' I said.

'Oh Hen, even I surprised myself.'

'Kitty,' I said. 'Do tell, for I think I might burst with curiosity.'

Kitty beamed. 'Why Hen, I do believe I have fallen in love.'

'In love?' I said.

'His name is Albert,' said Kitty.

'Albert?' I said.

'Oh Hen, are you going to repeat everything I say?' said Kitty. 'Why, you sound like a parrot.'

I laughed. 'But Kitty, I thought you would never get married.'

'Who said anything about marriage?' She pulled me along. 'Come, let us keep walking while I tell you the story.'

And so we walked across the park and I became quite lost in Kitty's travels.

'It was going so well,' said Kitty. 'The roads south of London were surprisingly dry. I had made about thirty miles or so by lunchtime and was quite flying along when I must've pedalled over a spike, for my front tyre became quite flat and I could not cycle on. I had to push for a fair few miles and I was hungry and thirsty when I arrived in the town of Haywards Heath.

I was thinking of taking the train back to London when a young man, not much older than myself, approached me. He was quite covered in soot and oil. He asked if I needed assistance and offered to look at my bicycle as he himself had an interest in them. He said he was a stoker, one of the people who shovel coal into the steam engine to keep it moving, but that he wanted to become an engineer one day. He had not guessed at my identity and thought he was addressing a young man.

It is quite remarkable being a man in a man's world, for suddenly you are elevated to his equal. He does not think your head is full of fluff and feathers. It is as if you have been cut free and allowed to take up space in the world. For the first time ever I felt I had become visible. When I showed an interest in the workings of the steam engine, he gave me a tour and explained about pistons and valves and the force of water and steam at different temperatures. He is so full of ideas. Why, he even said that one day we will invent carriages that will fly through the air and carry people across the world in a day.'

'Kitty!' I said. 'I think he has taken leave of his senses. How can a metal carriage carrying hundreds of people possibly fly into the air? It is quite impossible.'

'That's what I said to Albert,' said Kitty, 'but he said a hundred years ago steam trains and telephones and electricity would have seemed impossible too.'

'So how did he find out you are a woman?'

Kitty smiled. 'Albert mended my tyre with some bitumen and rubber he found at the station. He said it would be sufficient to see me back home although he suggested I travel by train. I quite forgot myself and asked if I could use the powder room and he appeared quite confused. I tried to cover my mistake but he had come to the realization that I was indeed a woman. I have never seen someone blush so deeply red as he did then. I was amused by his embarrassment, for by then we had already had quite the most interesting time. My train was pulling in to the station and I had to rush. I asked how I would find him if I needed a puncture repair again and he said he worked on the trains to Victoria Station. Just as my train was leaving the station, he ran along the platform. He said he would stand beneath the clock at Victoria Station at eleven o'clock next Tuesday.'

'Oh Kitty, you barely know him,' I said.

'I know,' said Kitty, 'but there is something about him. My heart pounds at the very thought of him.'

'Is he handsome?' I asked.

'He is not what some people call handsome,' said Kitty, 'but he has a kind face and when he smiles, his eyes light up. There is an energy and curiosity about him that I find intoxicating.'

'So shall you meet him next week?'

'Of course,' said Kitty. 'If I didn't, I think I would regret it for the rest of my life.'

At the doctor's house, Georgie and the Duchess teased Kitty mercilessly about Albert, but Kitty did not seem to care at all.

While we had tea, the Duchess explained that because so many people had responded to the letters we had delivered, Etta Smith had printed a small run of pamphlets to be pushed through people's doors. So this time, Kitty and I needed even bigger bags to carry on our bicycles. We finished our tea and cake and set out again, delivering pamphlets all around the borough.

We were both quite exhausted and red-faced by the time we had finished and we pushed the bicycles back through Regent's Park on our return. We sat down for a rest on a park bench. It was tucked away behind a bush and so it felt as if we were the only ones in the park.

Kitty, pulled her skirts up to her knees, closed her eyes, and turned her face up to the sun. I did the same and felt the glorious warmth seep beneath my skin.

'Do you think you shall try to ride to Brighton again?' I said.

'Maybe, maybe not,' said Kitty.

'Oh,' I said.

I think she could hear the disappointment in my voice. I opened my eyes and could see her looking at me.

'Oh Hen.' She held my hand and squeezed it tight. 'It doesn't matter if I get to Brighton or not. Some people are so intent on their destination that they forget to live. Don't you see? Life is such a grand adventure. We have to treasure each precious moment, like this one here with you, and hold it deep inside. We never know what might happen. We must remember to live every moment and enjoy the glory of the ride.'

'Henrietta!'

I turned to see Mother with two of her friends. They were all wearing their finest hats with long bright feathers and taking the air in the park. Mother was wearing the new hat with the green bird from Father.

'Henrietta, what are you doing? Cover up your legs at once.'

Kitty stood up. 'Josephine dear, we were running an errand for the Duchess of Portland.' She handed a spare pamphlet to one of Mother's friends.

'On bicycles?' snapped Mother.

'It is quite invigorating,' said Kitty. 'Perhaps you should try it too?'

Mother's mouth formed a thin hard line I see only when she is really cross.

She turned to me. 'You have exerted yourself, Henrietta. You are quite red-faced. This is no way to be seen as a lady.'

'Oh, Mother,' I ventured. 'It really is quite fun.'

Mother's face became quite purple. 'You will come home with me immediately.'

'Yes, Mother.'

She put her face so close to mine, closer than

she has for many years. 'And,' she said with such force her cheeks quivered, 'I never want to see you riding a bicycle again.'

Semira shut the diary and stared at it. It seemed that Hen's world and *her* world were so impossibly close as to be almost touching each other. How she wished she could reach through and be with her too.

CHAPTER 13

Semira met Patrick in the library at lunch the next day.

'Graham saved you a piece of cake,' he said, pushing a slice of cake wrapped in foil across the table. 'You didn't get to have your second slice.'

'Thanks,' said Semira, wolfing it down.

'Blimey,' said Patrick. 'You were hungry.'

Semira wiped her mouth with the back of her sleeve.

'By the way,' said Patrick. 'Graham and Mum said to ask if you want to come with us all on a bike ride on Saturday. We're training for the London to Brighton ride.'

'London to Brighton?' said Semira. 'That's about fifty miles.'

'We have to do the shorter ride from Haywards Heath because I'm under fourteen. It's so unfair. But we're just training this Saturday. We're doing about fifteen miles along a disused railway track.'

Semira knew Robel and Mama would never let her join Patrick and his family. But what if they didn't know? She'd have to work out a way to do it.

'I'd like to come,' she said. 'Thanks.'

'Good,' said Patrick. 'Come to ours at ten.'

Semira watched him leave as Holly and Chloe came in. Chloe looked red-faced and her eyes were puffy.

'Where were you at lunch?' said Holly. 'We were worried about you.'

'I brought some in,' said Semira, pointing to the empty foil. She looked at Chloe. 'Are you OK?'

Chloe shook her head. 'I haven't done my maths homework and Mr Jennings is going to kill me. I just don't get it.'

'There's no point copying mine,' said Holly. 'I think it's all wrong too. I didn't get it either.'

109

'You can both copy mine,' said Semira.

'Would you mind?' said Chloe. 'Mum and Dad will go mental if I move down a class.'

Semira glanced at the clock. 'We've got twenty minutes.'

She watched Chloe and Holly meticulously copy down her answers.

'I owe you big time,' said Chloe. 'You've literally just saved my life.'

'Me too,' said Holly. 'And just in time. There's the bell.'

Semira started packing her books away.

'Was Patrick bothering you when we came in?' said Holly.

Semira shook her head. 'Patrick's OK.'

Chloe smirked. 'Really? Doesn't he go on about birds all the time?'

'Yeah, a bit,' said Semira. 'It's fine though.'

Holly shrugged her shoulders. 'Well don't let Mad Dog and his mates know you're friends. They'll pick on you next.'

'Shouldn't we stick up for him?' said Semira.

'Only if you've got a death wish,' said Chloe. 'You don't know Mad Dog.'

Semira hurried home, her mind whirring about joining Patrick and his family on a bike ride the next day. She didn't have to make any excuse as she discovered that Robel would be taking Mama to a new job across the river. Getting to Patrick's would be easier than Semira had thought.

She woke early the next day and joined Robel and Mama for breakfast.

Robel gave Semira five pounds to get some lunch. 'What are you doing today?'

'Homework,' Semira lied. 'And I have books from school to read.'

'We'll be back about five,' said Robel.

'Be good,' said Mama.

Semira stood in the window watching them leave. The moment they turned the corner, she pulled on a coat and then ran to Patrick's house. She arrived just as Patrick and a woman in flowery Lycra leggings and a sports vest were loading up the bicycles onto a rack on the back of the car.

'You made it,' said Patrick. 'We were going

to go without you.'

'You must be Semira,' said the woman. 'I'm Debbie, Patrick's mum.'

'I'll get a bike for Semira,' said Graham. 'We'll have to put it on the roof.'

Semira stood back as Graham and Debbie heaved the last bike up.

'We've got plenty of food,' said Debbie. 'We hoped you'd come.'

Semira climbed in the car between Patrick and Lily and watched the houses whizz by, until the streets were replaced by fields and hedgerows.

'It's hard to find somewhere away from roads,' said Graham. He pulled into a car park by a canal. 'But we can cycle for miles here without meeting any cars.'

Debbie pushed things into her backpack and the saddlebags, while Graham unloaded the bikes.

Semira soon got used to riding the bike again. She followed the others along an old railway, through tunnels formed from overhanging branches and along a corridor of trees. The sunlight flashed between the tree trunks, and the ticking of the bicycle wheels lulled Semira into a steady rhythm. A canal ran alongside the railway and she spotted a tall grey bird standing like a statue on the canal bank.

'Heron,' said Patrick, pulling alongside her. 'And two cormorants over there.' He pointed to two black birds sitting on a barge boat, their wings outspread to the sun.

Graham and Debbie pulled up by a gate and peered over. 'Good picnic spot over here. Let's lift the bikes over.'

Semira helped them hide the bikes behind a hedge and they walked down to a river that ran parallel with the canal. The sky was blue and cloudless and the sun warmed Semira's skin. Graham was walking ahead with his arm around Lily.

'Is Graham your stepdad?' she asked.

Patrick nodded.

'Don't you miss your real dad?'

Patrick didn't answer for a while and Semira wished she hadn't asked. She knew what it was like to want to keep things inside.

Just before they reached the picnic spot, Patrick spoke. He pushed his hands deep in his pockets. 'My dad's got a temper. He's not allowed to see us any more. Mum said she'd never live with another bloke again, but then she bumped into Graham. Literally. She knocked him off his bike.'

Semira laughed out loud, but then covered her mouth. 'I'm sorry.'

'Don't be,' said Patrick. 'She went to see him in hospital to apologize and that's how they got together.

Semira watched Patrick join his family. Debbie spread out the picnic and started flapping her hands in the air. 'Come and join us Semira, grab a sandwich before the wasps eat all the picnic. I can't believe wasps are out so early in the year.'

Semira sat down with them and helped herself to some food. She had thought they were the perfect family. She had been jealous, almost, wanting what Patrick had; a home, food to eat, somewhere to feel safe. Yet, from what Patrick had said, she realized things hadn't always been easy for Patrick and his mum. Yet, here they now were, laughing and happy. Maybe things could be different for Semira and Mama too. Maybe.

After lunch they cycled slowly back while Lily raced ahead to wait and take photos of them as they passed.

'You should take up cycling,' said Graham to Semira. 'You're a natural.'

Semira smiled. Graham always seemed to say nice things.

'I mean it,' said Graham. 'You've got the biomechanics for it.'

'The what?'

'Biomechanics. You're like Patrick. You're long and lean.'

'Maybe,' said Semira.

'Come along to the cycle club next week,' he said. 'There's a junior meet.'

'I'd like to,' said Semira, 'but I don't have a bike.'

Graham took a swig of water from his water bottle and replaced it in the holder. 'I've just picked up some old bike frames free from the tip. You can choose one if you like and do it up.'

'I can't pay for repairs,' said Semira.

'Well, if you do a bit of oiling and painting for me, that can be payment.'

'Really?' said Semira.

'Did Patrick mention the Haywards Heath to Brighton ride?' said Debbie. 'Are you going to join us?'

'Can I do that?'

'It means you'll be stuck with us all day,' said Patrick.

Semira beamed. 'I'd love to come.'

Semira ran home. It was almost five, but she was relieved to find Mama and Robel hadn't returned. She rushed up to her room, pulled the diary out, and climbed into bed. She wanted to step through into the diary. She wanted to run down the cobbled street to Hen's house and tell her that she was planning to ride to Brighton, just like Kitty. Most of all, she wanted to tell Hen that she would have a bicycle of her very own.

CHAPTER 14

Wednesday 27th May, 1891

Dearest Friend,

I have not written for a little while, as I have had nothing of note to write about. Mother has not let me out of the house for a whole week now and I have been interminably bored. She has forbidden me to meet with Kitty and I feel quite bereft. I have had no means of sending a message to her. I desperately wanted to know about her meeting with Albert yesterday.

However, today things became a little brighter. The Duchess of Portland called at our house. Our house! Can you imagine? Mother was in quite a flap. The Duchess said she required my writing skills as she had some correspondence she wished me to write for her, and she had noted my neat hand.

Mother insisted that Mrs Tindall do my hair and squeeze me into a peach chiffon gown. Mrs Tindall pulled my hair a little too firmly and it took all my patience not to complain. I have noted that Mrs Tindall has seemed quite sour-tempered all this week and has not been baking quite up to her usual standard. Even Father noticed and has suggested that if things do not improve we may need to look for another housekeeper.

Before I climbed into the cab, Mrs Tindall pressed a small cake box into my hand. 'If you happen to see Miss Kitty, please give her this.'

I rode next to the Duchess but could not help taking a peek at the cake inside. It was a plain fruit cake, nothing unusual, but what I did notice were lots of names written inside the box. I saw the Duchess watching me and I quickly closed the lid.

We soon arrived at the doctor's house where Kitty and Etta were waiting for us.

'Kitty!' I exclaimed. I resisted throwing my arms around her. I wanted to ask about her meeting with Albert, but knew I would have to wait.

The Duchess smiled. 'I thought you might like to see your aunt.'

'I do,' I said. 'But do you not need my help?'

'Oh I do indeed, Henrietta,' she said. 'Now I have some rather wonderful news. In just a few weeks since our inaugural meeting of the Society for the Protection of Birds we have had a number of correspondences. She lifted a large cotton sack and tipped the contents out on the table.

It was full of letters.

'Just look,' said Etta. 'All these people have responded to our pamphlets. They all want to join us. And now we must get to work and file and answer each one.'

Etta carefully wrote down each person's address in a register and I wrote letters of receipt back to those who had sent or promised money.

'It's incredible, isn't it?' said Etta. 'We never realized so many people felt the same way about this issue.'

'It's just the same with women's votes,' said Kitty. 'There are many more who are simply too frightened to come forward.'

'Really, and how do you know?' said Etta sharply.

For the first time Kitty fell silent on the matter and I feel it was because there was something she would rather not say. As if she were hiding something.

'Women do not need the vote,' said Etta, 'because a good woman should have influence over a good man. He is there to serve and protect her.'

'But what if that man turns out not to be so good,' said Kitty, 'what then?'

'And what of your young man, Kitty?' teased the Duchess. 'Is he a good man?'

Kitty blushed and nodded. 'I believe Albert to be the best of men.'

'He must be a very brave one to take you on,' said Georgie.

'And does your good man think women should have the vote?' said Etta, glaring at Kitty.

'He agrees with it,' said Kitty. 'His mother and two sisters died in the workhouse. He believes that if she had been able to keep the tenanted farm after his father's death, his family would be alive today.'

'A woman farmer!' exclaimed Etta.

'Why not?' said Kitty. 'We are here to give a voice to the voiceless birds. Let's give our voice to women too. Now is the time to stand up and fight.'

'Women do not fight,' said Etta. 'We are different from men. Imagine if women started breaking the law and protesting to vote?'

'We have to question who makes the laws and who benefits from them.' said Kitty. 'How can we change the law if we cannot vote? Maybe the only way is to break it.'

'I disagree,' said Etta vehemently.

'We can't become criminals,' said the Duchess. 'Besides, it's irresponsible. Who would look after the children if mothers were in prison?'

Georgie raised an eyebrow. 'The problem with lawbreaking is that it gives more reason for men to refuse to give us a vote.'

'They know they have us exactly where they want us,' snapped Kitty. 'If we don't challenge it, nothing will change.'

'Well you're on your own,' said Etta.

'I have a group of women who will follow me,' said Kitty. 'I'm prepared to break the law.'

There was silence in the room while Kitty held her head up defiantly.

'Be very careful Kitty,' said the Duchess quietly. 'I cannot support you in this.'

Kitty stood up. 'Thank you for tea, but I must take my leave.' She strode out, leaving the sort of calm after a storm when the world has been left quite topsy-turvy.

I helped the Duchess finish the letters in sombre silence after that.

The Duchess accompanied me home. 'Kitty is a brave girl, if a little hot-headed at times. It may get her into trouble, but her reasons are just.'

Mother was waiting for the cab when we arrived home. She asked if the Duchess would care to take tea, but the Duchess said she was in rather a hurry.

Mother asked me what she had been talking to me about. I said how the Duchess is concerned for all the birds.

'But there are plenty,' Mother said.

'The Duchess thinks not,' I said. I gave Mother a pamphlet the Duchess had given me. 'She has lists of all the birds that are sold through London alone.'

Mother looked most concerned and called Father. 'Clarence, what do you think of this? The Duchess of Portland is calling for women to stop wearing feathers?'

Father read the pamphlet, a frown forming upon his face.

'Why would the Duchess do this?' cried Mother shrilly. 'She could influence the Queen. It would put us out of business, Clarence.' She clamped her hand against her heart. 'We could become destitute.'

Father put his hand on Mother's shoulder. 'Do not fret, my dear. It is just the sentimentality of women. It will blow over. There are so many birds. Leave this to the men who know what they are doing. I doubt any woman has travelled to these countries where the birds come from. I'm sure the men can decide if there are enough birds left.'

'Quite,' said Mother. 'Thank you for being sensible. I don't know how you cope with making such decisions.'

Father smiled. 'But you have important decisions too, my dear. Why, I would not know where to begin with running a household. What colour curtains, or cushions? Imagine my dear, if our roles were reversed, even for a day.'

Mother seemed to find this highly amusing and giggled with Father at such a notion. 'Suppose a woman could be Prime Minister,' she said. 'Why, she would have a beautiful house but a ruined country.'

'Well that won't happen, dear. Even today, I heard that a woman was put in prison for disrupting a council meeting. Silly fool was demanding women's votes.'

'Prison?' I said. I couldn't help interrupting their conversation.

'Yes, prison,' said Father.

'And quite right too,' agreed Mother. 'How can women entertain the thought of having a vote if they disobey and break the law?'

I climbed the stairs to bed feeling very heavy

in my soul. Kitty was up to something, I could tell. She wasn't afraid of anyone or anything. I wanted to warn her. I wanted her to stop whatever she was planning. But I feared my warnings would not change her mind at all.

CHAPTER 15

Over the next week, Semira stopped at Patrick's house after school to work on the bike. She couldn't stop for more than an hour or Robel would become suspicious. She had chosen a bike frame that was a little too big for her, but one that Graham said she would grow into. It had been a racing bike once, with sleek lines and a light frame. Graham helped Semira to fix the handlebars and choose the pedals. The wheels weren't too buckled, but they needed new tyres. Semira found she loved creating a machine from an unwanted frame. New words filled her language; derailleurs, sprockets, and cranks. She learned how to change a wheel and adjust brakes. It was like giving new life to something. She began to dream of where she and the bike would go. Maybe London to Brighton. Then London to the rest of the world.

She loved her afternoons after school with Patrick, but dreaded the weekends, because she knew she would be stuck in the house with Robel. Mama never wanted to go out anywhere, and Robel often had work lined up for her to do. So Semira was frustrated that Saturday had come around so soon. She sat down with her mother for breakfast. She wanted to go to Patrick's house and work on the bike, but she knew Robel wouldn't let her go out on her own.

'Why don't we go to the park today, Mama, just you and me?'

'Maybe,' said Mama.

Abdul walked into the kitchen and made himself a coffee. 'Hello, Semira.'

'Hello, Abdul.'

'I thought I'd let you know I am moving on next week. There is a construction job in a town somewhere north of London.'

'That's good,' Semira said.

'You take care,' said Abdul. 'Take care of your Mama.'

'I will,' said Semira.

'Semira,' Mama whispered. 'Don't talk to the others here.'

Semira slipped into speaking Tigrinya. 'Abdul is the one who leaves us flour to make bread, Mama. He feeds me breakfast when Robel hides the food.'

Mama stared at her own hands. 'You must let him know that we thank him very much.'

'What are you doing today?' said Abdul.

'We might go to the park,' said Semira.

Abdul reached into his pocket and put a five-pound note on the table. 'Here. Buy yourselves an ice cream each.'

Semira couldn't help smiling.

But Mama pushed the note back across the table. 'Tell him we can't accept any money.'

'I insist,' said Abdul. 'He gave the note to Semira and walked upstairs with his coffee. 'I hear the chocolate ice cream is the best,' he called down.

Semira grinned. 'Oh Mama. Let's go and eat ice cream in the park today. You and me. We can sit in the sunshine. There is a lake we can go to and watch the birds too.'

Mama smiled and held Semira's hands. 'Yes. Why not? A day out for the two of us.'

Robel walked into the kitchen as Semira and Mama were washing up.

'I have a job for you,' he said to Mama. 'It pays well. We are going to work at the café in the park. A friend is the manager there. He needs me to cover today. He says you can clear tables and work in the kitchen.

'We're going out today,' said Semira. 'Together.'

'Well you're not now,' said Robel. He turned to Mama. 'Ten minutes. Be ready.'

'Mama, tell him we're going out. He can't tell us what to do.'

Mama sighed. 'We need the money. Please take my bag upstairs. Make sure you put it under the bed and lock the door.'

Semira did as Mama asked, though she

couldn't imagine anyone wanting to steal her old bag.

'What time will you be back?' asked Semira.

Mama shrugged her shoulders. 'I think we will be there most of the day.'

Semira watched them leave. There was no way she was going to stay in the house today. She waited until after they had left and headed towards Patrick's house. At least she could work on her bike today.

'You're almost done,' said Graham. 'You just need new brake blocks and a touch of paint and you're ready to go.'

Semira fitted new brake blocks and oiled the chain one last time.

'Looks great,' said Lily. 'What are you going to call it?'

Semira frowned. 'Call it?'

'Yes,' said Lily. 'You have to give it a name. It makes you belong to each other. Mine's called Comet. That's why I painted him yellow.'

'I don't know,' said Semira. 'I'll have to think.'

'You should give it a test ride,' said Graham. 'Why don't you and Patrick go to the park?'

'I'll get my bike too,' said Patrick.

Semira walked her bike along the road to the park behind Patrick. It wasn't just any bike. It was her very own bike. The one she had made. She knew every bolt and chain link. She was about to ride it for the very first time.

'Ready?' said Patrick at the entrance to the park.

Semira nodded. She pushed off and felt the power in her muscles drive down through the pedal. It was as if she and the bike were one being. The ground slipped beneath them and the bike responded to every turn of her body. She felt bigger somehow, taller. Powerful.

She stopped beside Patrick at the top of the hill. Below she could see the park café. Mama would be in there, scraping food off plates and emptying and filling a dishwasher. She could see Robel at the front of the kiosk, serving customers. He hadn't seen her yet.

Semira looked at all the families in the park, the mothers and fathers walking hand in hand with children and eating ice creams. It wasn't fair. It wasn't fair that Robel wouldn't even let her and Mama have time to walk together in the park. She gripped her hands around the handlebars feeling fury flow right through her.

She couldn't take her eyes off Robel. 'Patrick,' she said. 'Do you want an ice cream? I've got some money.'

'Cool,' said Patrick.

Semira didn't wait for an answer.

'Semira, wait for me,' called Patrick, but Semira had already gone.

She pedalled down the hill towards the café, fixing her gaze on Robel. Faster and faster. All the anger surged through her, through the bike frame and into the wheels. At the last moment she pulled on her brakes and spun sideways, spraying grit into the air.

Robel looked up as Semira pulled off her cycle helmet.

He just stared at her.

Patrick pulled up behind her. 'Why so fast?'

But Semira left her bike on the ground and

walked up to the kiosk. 'Two ice creams,' she said. 'Chocolate, please.'

Robel said nothing and continued to stare.

'I said I would like two ice creams,' repeated Semira. 'Chocolate, please.'

A queue had begun to form behind her and Patrick came to stand beside her.

'Go home,' growled Robel under his breath.

'I would like two ice creams,' said Semira. She could see Mama behind Robel, watching from the small kitchen.

'Semira, go home,' repeated Robel.

'I would like two ice creams and I'm not leaving until I have them,' said Semira, raising her voice for others to hear. 'I am a customer. Your job is to serve *me*.'

Patrick frowned beside her. 'Is everything all right?'

Robel scooped chocolate ice cream into two cones and thrust them at Semira.

As she handed over the five-pound note, Robel grabbed her wrist. 'You'll regret this,' he hissed.

Semira pulled her hand from his, turned and

walked away, and did not look back, but knew Robel would be watching her leave.

Patrick followed Semira to the bikes then turned around. 'Who was that?'

'Robel,' said Semira.

'Is he your dad?'

'No.'

'Is he your stepdad?' said Patrick.

'No,' said Semira. 'I hate him.'

She lifted her bike from the ground and pushed it along with one hand, eating the ice cream with the other.

'He looks like he's got a temper,' said Patrick. 'Does he use it?'

Semira looked at him. 'He's never hit me, if that's what you mean.'

'Does he hurt your mum?'

Semira didn't answer. *Yes*, she wanted to say. *Mama thinks I don't know, but I've heard him do it. I have seen the bruises. I'm not stupid.*

'You can call the police you know,' said Patrick, 'if people hit you.'

'So why don't you tell the teachers about Mad Dog?'

Patrick frowned. 'I don't want Mum to know. She'd worry.'

Semira stayed silent. But perhaps, she thought, staying silent was the problem. A cloud had covered the sun and a chill wind blew across the park.

'Come on,' said Semira, 'let's get back.'

At Patrick's house, Semira washed the dirt from her bike and wheeled it into the garage. She felt smaller again, less powerful without it.

Graham and Debbie both insisted that they walk her home, but Semira refused. They both seemed concerned. Had Patrick said something to them? She reached the end of the street and turned to see his mum standing in the road, watching her leave.

As she walked back home, a hard rain was starting to fall.

She glanced through the railings as she walked past the park. Robel would be working still. She had been stupid to challenge him like that. It was easy to challenge him out the open. It was easier to be brave with lots of people around. But back at home there would be nobody around at all. Robel would get his revenge when she was alone.

She knew she hadn't heard the last of this.

She climbed the stairs up to her room.

Feeling very scared and very small.

CHAPTER 16

Semira sat on the end of the bed, waiting.

Waiting.

She knew she may as well get it over with, but she felt a fear run right through her. She had never challenged Robel like that before.

She heard the front door open and Robel's feet thumping up the stairs followed by Mama's. He banged on the door.

'Unlock this door, Semira,' he shouted.

'It is not locked,' she said. She tried to keep her voice level and pretend she wasn't scared.

Robel burst through the door and stood in the centre of the room filling up all the space. 'Just what do you think you were doing today?'

'Cycling,' said Semira, 'like many other people in the park.'

'What did I say about cycling?' he said.

Semira folded her arms. 'You can't stop me.'

Mama pulled on Semira's sleeves. 'Hush, child, hush.'

Semira pulled herself free. 'I've agreed to do the London to Brighton ride with Patrick.'

Robel pressed his face close to hers. 'You will not do this. Do you understand me?'

Semira said nothing, but remained defiant.

'I am the one to look after you,' shouted Robel. 'I brought you all the way safely here. You would be dead without me. And this is how you repay me?'

'We don't need you,' said Semira calmly. 'We never have. It's you that needs us.'

Robel was silent then.

'And I will tell the authorities about you,' she said.

Semira wasn't ready for the slap on the face. It stung and made her eyes water. Mama stood up and placed herself between Robel and Semira. 'Hush, Semira, hush.' She was crying, trying to block Robel. 'Please leave, Robel. Semira is upset. She will say sorry when she has calmed down. Please leave.'

Semira looked behind her to see Abdul in the doorway, glaring at Robel.

Robel pushed past and went downstairs, banging his fist against the wall as he went.

Abdul looked in. 'Are you both OK?'

Mama was crying but Semira felt cold rage. 'Yes thank you, Abdul.'

She shut the door and locked it and sat back down on the bed.

'Semira,' wept Mama. 'Don't anger Robel. You must not ride in this race.'

'Why not, Mama? It's just a bicycle.'

'It's not just a bicycle, Semira,' said Mama. 'You have to understand that.'

'I don't understand, Mama. You never explain anything.'

Mama put her hands on Semira's shoulders. 'Do not anger Robel.'

Semira stood up. 'Why not? So he doesn't hit me harder next time? When does it stop?'

'Semira!'

'I hate him,' said Semira. 'Why is it that all men think they can do whatever they like?'

Mama shook her head. 'Not all men do, Semira. There are good men.'

'Name one,' snapped Semira.

Mama's eyes brimmed with tears. 'If I tell you, we could risk everything. If I tell you, it could destroy us all.'

CHAPTER 17

'Tell me,' said Semira. 'I have a right to know.'

Mama checked the door was locked and pushed the bed against it. 'Sit down,' she said. She kneeled by Semira and took her hands in hers. 'Your father was a good man, Semira.' Tears began to flow down her face. 'He was a very good man.'

Semira felt her world falling around her. Mama had never spoken about him before.

But Mama did not let go of Semira's hands. 'Your father was the man who blew your paper boat across the puddle-sea. *My little bird* he used to call you. *My little bird.* He loved you so much. He wanted to give you the world. Most of all he wanted you to have an education. He was a maths lecturer.' She smiled shyly. 'It is how we met. I beat him in a competition. He worked in a college and I was a primary school teacher at the time.'

'I don't understand,' said Semira. 'Why couldn't you have told me this before, what difference would it have made?'

'There was something else,' she said. 'Your father had another love too. He loved cycling. It is a big thing in Eritrea. Bicycles were brought over by the Italians many years ago and it's the most popular sport. Everyone cycles. Your father was on the national team, training for the Olympics.'

'The Olympics?' said Semira. 'He went to the Olympics?'

Mama shook her head. 'He was on the team, but two cyclists escaped to America when they went for a competition there. And so the police watched your father and other team members very closely and wouldn't let them leave the country in case they tried to escape too. Your father tried to stand up against the government but he was arrested.'

Semira's eyes opened wide. 'Is he alive?'

Mama shook her head and closed her eyes. 'I don't know. I just don't know. I asked but was met by a wall of silence. There is no way of finding out.'

'How could you leave without knowing?' said Semira. 'How can you love someone and leave them like that?'

Mama sighed. 'The day your father was arrested he made me promise that I would get you out of Eritrea by any means. I have got you to freedom. I have kept my promise.'

'But why couldn't you tell me?'

'Because you were young. You might have told the authorities. If it became known we made it to England your father might never be freed. I couldn't risk it.'

'But why do we need Robel?' said Semira.

'I was scared, Semira. Being with Robel gave me some protection to get here. You too.'

'He hits you, Mama. Why did you stay with him?'

Mama sighed. 'If you were escaping a river

of crocodiles, wouldn't you try to ride on one's back?'

'We don't need him now,' said Semira.

'If the authorities find out we lied and that Robel is not my husband, they will send us back.'

'But who says that?'

'Robel does,' said Mama.

Semira got up and paced to the window. 'Maybe Robel tells us that. Maybe that's why he keeps you away from anyone who speaks your language. He controls us to keep himself safe.'

'But how can I know that, Semira?' said Mama. 'How can I know we won't be sent back?'

'We have to be brave,' said Semira.

Mama shook her head. 'But how?'

'Because many have been brave before us,' said Semira. 'Listen, Mama, I want you to meet someone. She reached under her pile of clothes and pulled out the cloth-bound book. '*The Feather Diaries*,' she said. 'I want you to meet Kitty and Hen.' She opened the book and began from the very beginning, translating into Tigrinya for Mama to understand.

She paused when she reached the end of the last entry she had read. 'This is where I got to. I don't know what happens now.'

Mama pulled the duvet over them and wrapped her arms around Semira. 'Let's read on, together.'

Tuesday 2nd June, 1891

Dearest Friend,

I am in now in my room and feel most fearful. There had been some commotion earlier. Father returned from work early accompanied by two policemen. I saw them in their bobby-blue uniform as I sneaked into the scullery. It is easy to hear conversation in the parlour from there. The sound travels down the chute for the dumb waiter. I thought maybe the police were here because someone had died. I sat perfectly still and tried to listen.

This is what I heard. I have tried to write the

important points down, word for word.

'We have a complaint against Miss Katherine Waterman,' said one policeman.

'My sister?' said Father. 'What has she done?'

'She has been arrested for causing an obstruction to a council meeting,' said the other policeman. 'She was demonstrating for votes for women. She threw eggs at the councillor.'

I heard Mother enter. 'Clarence dear, what has happened?'

'It is Katherine,' he said. 'She has been arrested. She was demanding women's votes.'

There was a loud scraping sound of someone pulling out a chair. 'Sit down my dear. I shall find you some smelling salts.'

'Oh, Clarence,' wept Mother. 'She is an embarrassment to this family. She has gone too far. I always said you were too lenient with her.'

'We have reports of a young man accompanying her, a stoker by the name of Albert Wells. He works on the Victoria line,' said the first policeman.

'I will have a word with the owner of the railway and ask for this Albert's immediate dismissal,' said Father.

'The shame of it,' cried Mother. 'She goes around in breeches, and a boy hanging off her arm. She must be stopped, Clarence. It does no good for my nerves. I fear she might influence Henrietta too.'

I could hear Father pacing the room. Then he said, 'I shall come to the station, and then we can decide the best course of action.'

I heard them leave and then crept out of the scullery. Mrs Tindall was rolling pastry. She looked at me. 'Snooping were you, Miss Henrietta? I reckon you heard all that.'

I was quite taken aback. If I'd had my wits about me, I would have accused her of the same thing.

She thumped the rolling pin on the table. 'Seems to me you're fond of your Aunt Katherine.'

I felt fierce pride burn inside. 'I am,' I said to her. 'I am very proud. She does not deserve to go to prison.'

Mrs Tindall came across to me then, wiping her floury hands on her apron. 'Oh Miss Henrietta,' she said. She wrapped her arms around me and was quite overcome with emotion.

'She's a brave lass, that Miss Kitty. You mark my words. It's ones like her that'll change the world for us women.' Mrs Tindall released me and dabbed at a tear on her face. 'I sometimes have a fancy of my own. In my fancies, I'm a chef with my own restaurant, creating the most marvellous cakes, where people come from far and wide to try them. Just imagine that, Miss Henrietta.'

'I should think everyone would like your cake, Mrs Tindall,' I said. 'It would be the talk of the town.'

She smiled and shook her head. 'I've said too much. I shouldn't think your mother would like to hear such talk.'

I could see she was fearful that I would report to Mother. 'There are many things I choose not to tell Mother,' I said.

I went to my room full of such confusing thoughts. I had never given much concern for the thoughts of the Mrs Tindalls of the world. I had assumed they were happy with their lot, honoured even to serve our family. But now I realize how stuck we all are in our society. Some are stuck by their birthright and others stuck by their fear of change, of giving up their power and privilege. Suppose Mrs Tindall could run her own restaurant. She would be free to choose her own path. All the Mrs Tindalls of the world could have their hopes and dreams. And it made me think something else too. If so many people think the same, then it only takes one brave person to open up the way ahead.

It takes one to be as brave as a lion, like my own dear Kitty.

CHAPTER 18

Semira closed the diary. 'You see, Mama. We have to be brave too. We have to stand up to him. We can live without Robel. We must be ourselves. You must learn English too.'

Mama held the book in her hands, turning the pages and looking at the words she could not read. She traced her fingers across the letters. 'This is even a different alphabet, Semira. How will I learn this?'

'Let me teach you,' said Semira. 'I'll bring books back from the school library. We'll go slowly, like you do with my maths. We can teach each other.'

Mama smiled. 'I will try. I will try it for you.'

'We must leave Robel,' insisted Semira. 'We

can do it. You and me. Just imagine, Mama. What if Papa is still alive? What if we could see him again?'

Mama put her hand on Semira's arm. 'Don't hold false hope.' She closed her eyes. 'Once people are arrested, they just go missing. No one can find out what has happened to them. I have to accept that we may never know.'

Semira held onto Mama's hands. They felt small and bird-like, yet Semira realized Mama hadn't just been brave to make the journey from Eritrea. It was more than that. She had to hold the loss of Semira's father inside her every day too.

Semira walked to school absorbed in her thoughts. The man blowing the paper boat had been her father. She could hear his voice, but however much she searched she couldn't see his face.

She had been loved by him, she thought. She had been loved.

Somehow just knowing that, made her feel

strong. The warmth from it spread through her like sunshine.

'Hey, Semira!'

Semira looked around. Holly and Chloe were walking behind her.

'Have you revised for the maths test?' said Chloe.

Semira nodded. It had been hard, but Mama had helped her with it.

'I'm going to fail,' said Chloe miserably. 'I just don't get it. Every time I try to get Mr Jennings to explain it again he just says it the same way but louder.'

'I could try and explain,' said Semira.

'You can try,' said Chloe. 'But I don't think I'll ever get it. I just can't do maths.'

Semira sat with them in the library at break and tried to explain the maths the way Mama had done with her. She gave them easy questions then harder ones. Chloe sat back and stared at her workbook. 'I actually get it,' she said. 'Why couldn't Mr Jennings explain it like that?'

'My mum taught me,' said Semira. 'She says

everyone can understand maths. They just have to find a way to suit them.'

'Cool,' said Holly. 'Can she teach us too?'

Semira smiled. She thought how Mama would love to teach maths here. It was an impossible thought.

'Right,' said Chloe, 'there's the bell. Time to go. Good luck.'

Semira sat through the maths test, looking sideways to see if Holly or Chloe were struggling, but they both had their heads down.

At the end of the test, Mr Jennings gathered the test papers in and then handed them back out randomly. 'Mark the paper you have in front of you when I read out the answers.'

Semira marked the one she had and then Mr Jennings collected them in and handed them back to their owners. He stopped beside Chloe and peered at the paper before handing it back. 'Are there two Chloe Clarkes in this class?'

Chloe frowned. 'No sir.'

He held it in front of her. 'Is this your work?'

Chloe looked at it. 'Yes.'

'Well done,' he said, grudgingly. 'Full marks.'

Semira joined Holly and Chloe outside after lunch.

They spread their blazers on the ground and sat against a wall, letting the spring sunshine warm their faces.

'Well done on the maths test,' said Semira.

'It's thanks to you,' said Chloe. 'Mr Jennings has no faith in me though. He obviously thinks there's more chance of two Chloe Clarkes in the room than me passing a maths test.'

'Watch out!' warned Holly. 'Incoming Bird Nerd.'

Semira looked up to see Patrick walking over. He stopped in front of them, clutching his bag and shifting from foot to foot. 'You OK?' she asked.

Patrick reached into his bag and pulled out a sheet of paper. He thrust it at Semira. 'Graham says you have to get your mum to sign it to give permission to come on the bike ride with us.'

Semira took the form from him, folded it, and put it in her bag. 'Thanks,' she said. She wanted to ask him more about the ride, but it would have been awkward talking about it in front of Holly and Chloe. She knew Patrick would have thought so too.

Silence filled the space between them until Patrick turned and shuffled away.

Holly watched him go. 'Are you really going on a bike ride with him?'

Semira nodded. 'And with his family. His stepdad is mad on bikes.'

Chloe sat up and brushed dirt from her skirt. 'Does he ever talk about his real dad to you?'

'Not much,' said Semira.

Holly leaned in closer. 'When we were at primary school he left school suddenly in year five. Then he turned up here in year seven in September with his mum as if nothing had happened. Only he came back without his dad. He never said what happened. There were rumours that his dad had died . . .'

'Or went to prison,' said Chloe. 'But no one

ever really knew. My mum said she'd never liked his dad.'

'He never had any friends round at primary school, did he?' said Holly. 'I remember he invited some of us for a party, but Mum didn't want me to go.'

'What's his stepdad like?' asked Chloe.

'Graham's nice,' said Semira. 'He makes good cake.'

Semira watched Patrick cross to the other side of the playground and sit by himself at a bench in the shade, placing his lunchbox and drink on the table. He was hunched, head down, and very different from the Patrick on the bike or at the bird reserve. As she was watching, she saw Mad Dog and a couple of his friends walk towards Patrick. They sat at the bench, and Mad Dog helped himself to one of Patrick's sandwiches. Patrick just sat while Mad Dog took another.

Semira glanced at Holly and Chloe. They had seen too.

'We can't let them do it,' said Semira.

'Leave it,' said Holly.

'We can tell one of the teachers,' insisted Semira.

'The teachers know,' said Chloe. 'They don't do anything about it. It only makes it worse.'

Semira looked around to see if there was a teacher on duty. A few people glanced in Patrick's direction then hurriedly looked away. No one went to help.

Semira thought of Kitty, being brave, standing up for others. *Be brave*, Semira told herself. *It just takes one person to be brave.*

'I'm going,' she said.

She could hear Holly and Chloe call her back, but she kept walking across the playground, her heart pounding inside her chest. She stood beside Patrick.

'Leave him alone,' she said.

Mad Dog turned to look at her.

'Do what?'

'Leave him alone,' said Semira, trying to stop her voice from trembling.

'It's OK,' said Patrick.

'It's not OK,' said Semira.

Mad Dog leaned closer. 'Says who?'

'Says us,' said a voice behind Semira.

Semira spun around. Holly and Chloe were standing there.

'Ooh!' laughed Mad Dog. 'Little Patrick needs three girls to protect him.'

'And you think that three of you against one is fair?' said Semira.

Mad Dog looked at them all and took a back step. He turned to Semira. 'Why don't you just go back to where you came from? No one wants your sort here.'

'Get lost, Mad Dog,' said Holly. 'We don't want *you* here.'

One of Mad Dog's mates pressed his face near Semira's. 'My dad says you lot are taking our jobs. You're just sponging off this country. You only came for the money.'

'Yeah,' said Mad Dog. 'I bet your mum and dad are laughing now.'

'Shut up,' said Semira.

'Oooh!' teased Mad Dog. 'Hit a raw nerve there. Where's Daddy now? Lazing about collecting benefits?'

'Shut up!' shouted Semira. She pushed past them. She could hear Patrick and Holly call her name but she wanted to get away. She didn't want them to see her cry. She ran to the library and sat down in the corner and tried to hide her face. Where was her father? She needed him now more than ever. She didn't even know his name. Surely she could find him.

She logged on to a computer and typed furiously on the search bar. 'Eritrean Olympic Cycling Team.'

There were lots of images of cyclists wearing the red, yellow, green, and blue of the Eritrean flag. Most were wearing cycle helmets and sunglasses and so it was difficult to see their faces. She clicked on the small image of three cyclists on a podium, holding up medals. The image filled the screen. She couldn't take her eyes from the cyclist in the middle of the podium. He was tall, long-limbed and lean. He had one of the widest smiles she had ever seen.

She felt a rush of recognition.

She knew this face.

Fierce love.

Blue sky. Red earth. Wide puddle. Little bird.

Little bird.

Little bird.

Little bird.

Semira's world was spinning, and falling in. She was sobbing but her voice sounded so far away, as if it were separate from her. She became aware of Patrick and the librarian ushering her into the librarian's office. Someone was pressing a biscuit and glass of orange juice into her hand. But she closed her eyes tightly and buried her head in her arms and sobbed.

All she could say over and over was;

'My papa.

My papa.

My papa.'

CHAPTER 19

Semira refused to let the school contact Robel or Mama.

The head teacher looked concerned but allowed Semira to sit in the library until the end of school when Patrick came to find her at home time. 'Come home with me. Mum's here with the car.'

Semira shook her head. 'No, I have to see Mama.'

'Mum wants you to come back,' Patrick insisted. 'You have to.'

Semira drove back with Patrick and Debbie. Graham was sitting in the kitchen drinking tea. One of Graham's homemade cakes lay on the table.

'Cake?' said Graham.

Semira sat down and let Graham put a piece of cake in front of her.

Debbie sat down beside her. 'Thank you for standing up for Patrick today. It was a brave thing to do. I had no idea what has been going on.'

'It won't make a difference,' said Semira.

'Of course it will,' said Debbie. 'I'll make sure it does.'

Semira picked at the cake. She didn't feel hungry. She closed her eyes and felt all the energy drain out of her.

'Patrick said you were very upset today.'

Semira put her head in her hands. 'Those boys said some nasty stuff. I'm over it.'

'I don't mean that,' said Debbie. 'Patrick said you were upset about something else. Your dad?'

Semira didn't know what to say or do. She wanted to go home, but she also wanted to stay. She wanted to talk about her dad with someone.

'You don't have to talk about it,' said Debbie.

'But we are here if you do.'

Semira sat up and nibbled at the cake, but her mouth had become dry and it was hard to swallow. 'He was a cyclist,' she said. 'He cycled for Eritrea.'

Graham smiled. 'It's in the genes,' he said. 'I thought you were a bit of a natural.'

Semira looked up. 'I never knew until yesterday. I never knew anything about him.'

No one spoke.

Semira stared at her hands. 'I haven't seen his face since we left Eritrea. I thought I couldn't remember what he looked like. But when I saw his photo, I knew it was him. I recognized him. Or at least, my heart did.'

Debbie took a sip of tea. 'Where is he now?'

'He was arrested,' said Semira. 'He's still in Eritrea.'

'No he isn't,' said Patrick.

Debbie frowned. 'What are you talking about, Patrick?'

Patrick went bright red. 'I didn't mean to,' he said. 'But I read the whole article you were reading in the library. You left it on the computer.'

'What d'you mean?' said Semira.

'Well the article was about the cyclists on the podium. It said they had all escaped to a refugee camp in Ethiopia.'

Semira just stared at him. 'I need to see,' she said.

'Wait,' said Graham.

But Semira had crossed the room to the family computer. She found the page again and read it. The date was from five years before. She read and re-read the words.

'His name is Isaac,' she said. 'Isaac Soloman.'

Debbie sat next to her. 'Wait a minute, Semira. Take time. Think what you want to know. This might be too big to deal with right now.'

'I want to find my father,' said Semira. She didn't take her eyes from the screen and typed his name again and again into the computer. There were many with the same name, but she couldn't find him. There was no sign of him. Nothing. It was as if he had vanished from the face of the earth.

But he had escaped.

He had escaped to Ethiopia.

He could be anywhere by now.

What if she could find him?

Semira could feel her heart thumping deep inside her chest.

What if?

What if?

What if?

What if Papa could still be alive?

What if he was looking for her too?

CHAPTER 20

Debbie insisted on driving Semira home.

'What can we do, Semira? I think you need to get someone to help you with this.'

'No,' said Semira. 'It's too complicated. No one must know.'

They drove in silence, the only words being Semira's directions.

'Please stop here,' said Semira. 'The house where I live is at the end of the street.'

Debbie pulled in to the side. 'Will someone be home for you?'

'Mama will be in,' said Semira.

Debbie turned to look at her. 'Patrick says there is someone, a man who is with you. Robel?'

Semira stared ahead and nodded.

'He said something that worries me,' said Debbie. 'He said he has a temper.'

'I have to go,' said Semira, unbuckling her seatbelt.

'Wait,' said Debbie. 'I know it might not be my business, but if you need help you must call us.'

Semira stayed silent.

'Patrick's father has a temper. He is not allowed contact with us now,' said Debbie. 'Staying silent only makes it worse.'

'But what can we do? No one would listen to us?' said Semira. She blinked back the tears.

'I'm listening,' said Debbie. 'And that's a start. I remember feeling the same. Patrick and I ended up in a women's refuge together when I left Patrick's father. When I found people who listened I knew we could get through it. It's hard. I know what it's like. Patrick does too. At school other kids pick on him for being sensitive and a bit different. Some kids are so lucky they don't have to live through

difficult times. Maybe they'd be a bit kinder
to Patrick if they knew.'

'I have to go,' said Semira. She climbed out
and shut the car door.

Debbie opened the window. 'If you ever
need help, you come to us. You can stay while
you find somewhere else. I mean it, Semira.
You can come to us, any time of day or
night.'

Semira let herself into the house and walked
slowly up the stairs.

Abdul put his head around the door. 'Robel
was looking for you. Did he find you?'

Semira shook her head. 'What did he want?'

'He said something about meeting up with
the immigration officers for an interview and
to sign some forms,' said Abdul.

She sat on the bed. She didn't know the
interview was happening today. She should
have come home early. She should have
stopped Mama signing the forms.

She felt exhausted. She'd challenged Patrick's
bullies, but could she challenge Robel?

What would Hen do? What would Kitty do?

She curled up on the bed, opened the diary, and began to read.

Wednesday 3rd June, 1891

Dearest Friend,

I fear the whole world has turned quite mad.

This evening Mrs Tindall knocked on my door and came in, shutting it behind her. She looked quite agitated.

'Miss Henrietta,' she said. 'I should tell you that I overheard a conversation that Miss Katherine is to come here presently. There is something up, I fear. I heard your father talking about a hospital.'

'Is she ill?' I said. 'Has she been hurt?'

'I fear your father thinks she needs a rest in a hospital to restore her senses.'

'You mean she is to be sent to a lunatic asylum? A madhouse, for mad people?' I said.

Mrs Tindall grasped my hands. 'Yes my dear. And it is a sad truth that those who go in there don't often get out.' She clutched my arm. 'There's the doorbell. I must rush.'

I ran down after her and went into the parlour where Father brought in Kitty. Georgie accompanied her in.

Mother was in the parlour too. There was something triumphant in Mother's manner.

'Ah Henrietta,' said Mother. 'I was going to call Mrs Tindall to come and fetch you.'

I looked at Kitty but she seemed subdued.

Mother flicked some dust from her skirts. 'You won't be seeing Aunt Katherine for a while and she wishes to say goodbye. She has agreed to take a rest in a hospital to reduce her hysterical nature.'

I looked at Kitty, and I could see tears welling up in her eyes.

'Aunt Kitty?' I whispered.

'What will be, will be, Hen dear,' she said.

'No,' I said. 'Don't go. They want to send you to a madhouse.'

Georgie looked at me. 'Don't call it that, Miss Henrietta,' she said kindly. 'One day there will be better treatments for people who suffer diseases of the mind. There will be more understanding too.'

'But Kitty isn't mad,' I shouted.

'Enough Henrietta,' snapped Mother.

Georgie tipped her head to the side. 'Sometimes I think there are more sane people on the inside than on the outside.'

Mother glared at Georgie then turned to me. 'Henrietta, say goodbye to your aunt.'

I turned to Georgie. 'You're her friend,' I implored. 'You can't let them take her.'

Georgie held my hands in hers. 'I have no choice.'

Mother raised her voice. 'Say goodbye to your aunt.'

Kitty seemed quite withdrawn. I gave her a peck on the cheek and put my arms around her, but she did not return my embrace at all. I curtsied and watched her leave.

I wanted to scream.

I wanted to shout.

She was my hope.

She was Mrs Tindall's hope.

But Kitty Waterman had given up.

My fierce, darling Kitty, who I thought was unbreakable, had just been broken.

CHAPTER 21

Semira looked up from the diary. She could hear arguing coming from downstairs. There were shouts and the sound of a plate breaking. She could hear Mama's voice, soft and calling for calm. She crept down and peered into the kitchen, wishing Abdul was around for safety. She could see Mama standing next to the sink. Robel was hovering over her and the smashed plate lay on the floor beside her.

'Go back to your room, Semira,' said Mama.

Robel spun around to look at her.

Semira took a step into the room. 'Leave Mama alone.'

Robel picked up a sheaf of papers, waving

them in her face. 'This is your fault, you stupid girl.'

'What is?'

Robel slammed the papers down on the table. He pointed at Mama and said in English: 'She won't sign until you have read it to her.'

Semira picked them up. 'What are they?' she said.

Robel glared at her. 'They are the documents to say we are a family and to apply for residence.'

'You haven't signed?' Semira said to Mama. 'You have not said you are Robel's wife yet?'

Mama shook her head.

Semira's heart soared. She felt so proud of Mama just then. She felt a lion's roar build up inside her. 'She will never sign.'

Robel smiled sourly. 'And who will look after you? You need me. I am your father now.'

Semira shook her head. 'No, you'll never be my father. Isaac Soloman is my father. He always will be.'

Robel just stared at her. 'Your father is in prison,' he said. 'He is as good as dead.'

'He isn't in prison,' said Semira.

Robel narrowed his eyes.

'And you knew,' she said. 'You've known for a long time.'

'Semira, what are you talking about?' said Mama.

Semira folded her arms. 'Papa escaped to Ethiopia five years ago.'

'It makes no difference,' said Robel. He pointed his finger in her face. 'You can't survive without me.'

'We can,' Semira said, 'and that's what we are going to do.' She grabbed Mama and pulled her out of the kitchen.

'Come back,' yelled Robel.

But Semira and Mama ran up the stairs and pushed the door shut, locking it behind them.

Robel's feet pounded behind them. He banged his fist on the door. 'Let me in! Let me in!'

Mama pushed the bed against the door. She turned to Semira. 'How do you know his name?'

'I saw him on a computer, but I don't know where he is. All it said was he made it to Ethiopia.'

Mama was silent.

'He escaped, Mama. He could be alive. He could be here in London.'

Mama looked at her. 'It is a long, long journey and I saw many dead on the way.'

'But he might be alive,' said Semira.

'Maybe.' She closed her eyes. 'Oh Semira. I need some courage.'

Robel banged on the door again. 'Let me in.'

Mama pulled Semira to sit down beside her. 'We are stuck here until Robel calms down. Why don't you read me the diary? It will help us to think of something else. It might give us courage too.'

Semira picked it up. 'It doesn't go well for Kitty. She has given up hope.'

'Read it to me anyway,' said Mama.

And so Semira read on . . .

I watched Georgie escort Kitty to the door. I felt my world caving in. I could not think of a world without Kitty.

I glared at Mother and Father. Mother looked so smug, like a cat that has got the cream. All of the cream. I hated her then. I hated her more than Father.

Just as I was about to run to my room, Mrs Tindall bustled back inside. She lifted something from behind the chair where Georgie had been sitting. 'Miss Henrietta dear, the doctor has asked that you fetch her umbrella. She left it here. Be quick, the cab is waiting.'

I grabbed the umbrella. I thought how strange that it was not raining and yet she chose to bring one.

I climbed in the cab and Kitty flung her arms around me.

'I'm so sorry,' she wept. 'My dear Hen, I'm so sorry.'

'Oh Kitty,' I said. 'Don't let them take you.'

'Oh Hen, I'm not. Did you ever think I would?'

'What do you mean?' I said.

'I am leaving,' said Kitty. 'My only great sadness and the reason that I am weeping is that I shall miss you, my darling Hen. I love you so very much. You have become a sister to me.'

'Where shall you go?'

'Why Hen, it is so exciting,' said Kitty, taking both my hands in hers. 'Albert lost his job. Your father made sure of that. But, he has been offered a new job on the railways in Africa, and I am joining him. Oh Hen, the places we'll go, the people we'll see, and all the animals and birds. Why I might even see an elephant and a lion. It shall be such a grand adventure. We are boarding the mail steamer from Southampton to Cape Town tomorrow.'

'But will you go dressed as a man?' I asked.

'No,' said Kitty. 'I am going as Albert's wife.' She slipped on a gold ring and showed it to me.

'And I thought you would never marry,' I said.

'I love him, Hen,' said Kitty. 'He is my equal, as I am his. The Duke and Duchess of Portland and Georgina were our witnesses.'

I could see the excitement in her eyes. 'But what about fighting for women's votes,' I said.

Kitty shook her head. 'I could stand and fight, but this is a battle I will surely lose. Your father can have me put in prison or hospital. I must pick my battles carefully, Hen. One day I will return and fight another battle in this war. We will win the right to have our vote one day. I'm quite sure.'

I held her so tightly. 'You will write, won't you. Please write.'

'Of course,' said Kitty. 'I shall send letters to Georgina or the Duchess, who shall make sure you receive them.' She stroked my hair. 'You can't get rid of me that easily, Hen. It's you and me, for ever.'

'For ever,' I said, weeping against her shoulder. I didn't want to let her go, but the horse was snorting and stamping its feet. The cab driver shouted in impatience.

I jumped down from the cab and watched her go.

'Godspeed,' I called to her as she left. 'Godspeed.'

And with that, she was gone.

She had escaped into the night.

Semira closed the book and she and Mama sat in solemn silence.

'It's what we need to do, Mama,' she said. 'We need to escape, too.'

Mama shook her head. 'But where would we go?'

'Pack your bags, Mama,' said Semira. 'We are leaving tonight.'

CHAPTER 22

Semira piled her clothes and schoolbooks into her holdall. There wasn't much to pack. She didn't want to leave the hat and the hatbox. She put the diary into the holdall as well and decided she would carry the hatbox under her arm.

Mama rolled up her clothes and put them in her old carpetbag. The leather straps had broken and the fabric was faded and ripped. It had survived the hot sun of the desert and the salt water of the sea.

'One day we'll get you a new bag,' said Semira.

Mama ran her hand over the bag. 'This means too much to me. It has seen many things.'

Semira pulled the bed away from the door, but she heard a movement outside. 'He's still there,' whispered Semira.

Mama held her ear against the door. 'We will have to wait,' she said.

'How long?' Semira said.

Mama sat back down and folded her hands into the lap. She was used to waiting. 'As long as it takes,' she said. 'We may not be able to leave for a while.'

Semira sat down next to her.

'Where are we going?' said Mama. 'I don't want to end up on the streets. We have no money. We have nothing.'

'We are going to friends,' said Semira.

'And what if they can't have us?' said Mama.

'Then we will find another way, Mama. We can't be ruled by Robel any longer.'

Semira watched the sky darken and the street lamps come on. She lay back on the bed and waited, listening to the hum of traffic and the occasional blare of a siren. She woke to Mama rocking her awake. 'Mama?'

'Hush, Semira. It is gone midnight. I think we are safe to leave.'

Mama opened the door just a crack and peered out. No one was there and the house was silent. She followed Mama down the stairs, keeping her feet away from the stairs' edge, so as not to make any creaking sounds. Mama opened the front door and they crept out into the night.

'This way,' said Semira.

She and Mama kept in the shadows close to the houses as much as possible. The park looked ominous as they passed and Semira hurried a little faster until they reached Patrick's house.

'This is it,' said Semira. It was late and dark. What if Debbie didn't really mean her offer of them staying there? What if it was just something people said to be polite? She could see Mama shivering.

Semira lifted her hand and knocked.

Lights came on, followed by footsteps and the rattling of the keychain across the lock.

'Who is it?' said Debbie.

'It's me. Semira. Can we come in?'

Debbie undid the keychain and opened the door. She looked at them both clutching their bags.

'Of course,' she said, ushering them in. 'Come into the warm.'

Graham came downstairs, bleary-eyed, in his pyjamas. 'Semira, what are you doing here?'

'They've come to stay,' said Debbie. 'Graham, you make them a cup of tea while I put a camp bed in the spare room.'

Graham fussed around Semira and her mother. He boiled the kettle and set mugs down on the table. 'The spare room's a bit of a mess, I'm afraid. I'll clear it out tomorrow.'

'Sorry,' said Semira.

'Don't be,' said Graham. 'Debbie's been on at me for ages to do it.' He made the tea and put a packet of biscuits on the table.

Semira wrapped her hands around the warm mug and inhaled the steam. Mama did the same and closed her eyes, and they sat there in the warm kitchen. It felt to Semira like a lull in the storm. A moment to think. A moment to breathe.

Debbie came downstairs. 'Right. Well that's the beds done for tonight. I've put towels in the bathroom for you. Try and get some sleep. We'll try to sort things out in the morning.'

Mama touched Semira's arm. 'Please thank them for me, Semira.'

Semira looked at Debbie and Graham. 'Mama says thank you.'

Debbie took Mama's hands in hers and looked her in the eyes. 'You're welcome.' She put her hand against her chest and said, 'My name is Debbie.'

Mama smiled and put her hand on her chest and said in English, 'my name is Hanna.'

Maybe there was some unwritten code that passed between them, because Mama put her arms around Debbie and they hugged each other for a long, long time.

'You are welcome here, Hanna,' said Debbie.

Semira just watched. It was the first time she had ever heard someone call Mama by her name.

Semira brushed her teeth and washed and then slipped into the camp bed between sheets that smelled new and clean. Mama lay in the bed beside her and they both lay awake listening to the sound of the house, of clocks ticking, the fridge buzzing, and the hot water burbling through the pipes.

'I am scared, Semira,' said Mama. 'I don't know what Robel might do.'

'I'm scared too, Mama,' said Semira. 'But I don't feel hopeless any more. We are being brave. Brave and fearless.'

'Sleep well, child.'

Semira stayed awake long after she heard Mama slip into sleep.

She wanted to stay awake and hold the moment.

It was a strange feeling, lying there between the four walls of Patrick's house.

For the first time she could ever remember, she felt safe.

CHAPTER 23

Semira woke to the sound of the washing machine spinning and doors slamming.

Debbie knocked on the door and put her head around. 'Patrick and Lily are just off to school. I've told school that you won't be going today. You were late to bed, and I think you need a day off while we sort a few things out. I think you'll need to translate a few things for your mum too.'

Semira dressed and went down to the kitchen with Mama to find another woman sitting at the table.

'This is a friend who can help,' said Debbie. 'Muriel used to work in immigration.'

Muriel sat with a computer and asked lots of

questions and filled in lots of forms. It turned out that Robel had been claiming money for Mama and holding on to it all.

'We see this a lot,' said Muriel. 'Some people know how to work the system. They especially prey on those who can't speak English.'

Semira translated this all and Mama sighed. 'I should have tried to learn.'

'It's not easy,' Muriel went on. 'People like Robel can be very controlling.'

'But will he come after us?' said Semira.

Muriel shook her head. 'I doubt it. Once these people know they've been detected they tend to disappear because they're scared they might be arrested and deported.'

'Will we be deported too?' said Semira.

'Unlikely, if your mother has been abused. But it's going to be tricky,' said Muriel. 'She's going to need to be prepared to tell her side of the story.'

'So Mama needs to learn to speak English,' said Semira.

Muriel smiled and pulled a leaflet from her bag. 'It will help. There's a class not far from here. It's about a thirty-minute walk. Hanna can start tomorrow.'

'Perfect,' said Semira. She pushed the leaflet towards Mama and spoke in Tigrinya. 'Tomorrow you are going to learn English.'

Mama picked up the leaflet and stared at it. She looked up and smiled. 'A new beginning, Semira. A new beginning for both of us.'

Semira thought it might be awkward for Patrick and Lily with her and Mama in the house, but they didn't seem to mind at all. She heard Patrick arrive home from school, dumping his bag in the hallway. He put his head around the kitchen door.

'Some people to see you,' he said.

Chloe and Holly followed him into the kitchen.

Patrick turned to his mum. 'You remember Holly and Chloe don't you?'

Debbie smiled. 'Of course.'

'I'll put the kettle on,' said Graham. 'You'll stay for a slice of cake won't you?'

Holly took a seat next to Semira. 'How are you?'

Semira glanced at Patrick and he went bright red.

'I've told them why you're staying with us for a while,' said Patrick. 'Sorry. They wanted to come and see you.'

'You should've told us,' said Chloe. 'We could've helped.'

'We wanted to check you were OK,' said Holly.

Semira stared at her hands. 'Thanks,' she said. 'What's happened to Mad Dog?'

'He's been suspended,' said Chloe, her eyes opening wide. 'After we went to the head, others came forward too. They'd been too scared to speak before.'

'Really?' said Semira.

'Yeah,' said Holly. 'Mad Dog and his mates were bullying loads of people for money.'

Debbie handed around pieces of cake. 'It just shows you have to stand up to them. Silence just gives them power.'

'You were brave, Semira,' said Chloe. 'Brave

or stupid. I thought you were going to get killed.'

'Me too,' said Semira. She smiled and thought of Kitty, brave as a lion, Kitty, who had given her courage.

Semira hadn't seen Mama slip into the room behind her.

'Are you Semira's mum?' said Holly.

Mama smiled at her.

'Oh my god,' said Chloe. 'You literally saved my life.' Semira turned to Mama and told her about the maths test they had done, and Mama replied to Semira in Tigrinya.

'Mama says she'd be happy to teach you once she has learned some English,' said Semira.

'And you are welcome here anytime,' said Debbie to Holly and Chloe.

'Thank you,' said Holly. She took a bite of cake and turned to Graham. 'Semira was right. This is amazing cake.'

That evening, Graham sat down at the table with a map and spread it out. 'I thought you'd like to see the route of the cycle ride to

Brighton.'

Semira peered over. 'Do you think I'm ready?'

Graham nodded. 'It's not too far from Haywards Heath to Brighton. We'll take it steadily. Besides, it's not a race. Our cycle club wants some photos to put in the local paper though. I have to send it tonight for it to be in the paper tomorrow. Do you want me to include you too? I have the photo from the other day on the canal towpath. The club wants to make a bit of a story about it.'

Semira frowned. 'If my father heard about me doing it, maybe he could find me.'

Graham looked at Debbie. 'Well, it's only a local paper.'

'But still,' said Semira, 'if I tell my story, and say I am the daughter of cyclist Isaac Soloman, maybe he will hear about it.'

'I don't know,' said Debbie. 'I'm not sure it's a good idea. The press doesn't like to put names of children. It's a protection thing.'

'They don't need to,' said Semira. 'Just say I am his daughter. Please! It might be the only way Papa can find me. It might be my only chance.'

Graham nodded. 'OK. But I'm not mentioning your name or where you live or anything about you, other than you are his daughter. Agreed?'

Semira nodded and felt hope well up inside her.

She couldn't stop thinking of her idea all night. Maybe Papa would read about her. He would discover that she would be finishing the ride in Brighton. Maybe he was in the UK right now. Maybe he would make his way to Brighton. In her mind, she imagined finishing the ride and seeing Papa with his arms outstretched, taking hold of her as she crossed the finish line. She replayed the dream time and time again in her head.

She woke the next morning to see Mama sitting on the end of her bed. Mama was up and dressed in some of Debbie's clothes; a pair of black jeans and a grey jumper with a bright-pink scarf.

Mama fiddled with the end of the scarf. She sighed. 'Debbie is taking me to the English class today.'

'But that's good, Mama.'

'But what if everyone is good at English already?'

'And what if they aren't?' said Semira.

Mama shook her head. 'What if I look stupid?'

'And what if you don't?' said Semira. 'Mama, you have nothing to lose and everything to gain.'

Semira pulled on her school uniform and went down for breakfast. Debbie looked across at Semira. 'Tell Hanna that I will take her there today so she knows the way. We can go on my way to work.'

Semira ate her breakfast as Mama came downstairs. Mama looked nervous, clutching the pen and exercise pad Debbie had given her. She reminded Semira of herself on the first day at a new school, the nervousness of meeting other people, the worry about fitting in.

Semira watched her walk out of the house.

If Mama could do this, then she could do anything.

Semira felt pride well up inside her.

Not even a week ago could she ever have dreamed of this happening.

Maybe dreams really could come true.

Maybe anything was possible.

Maybe she could see her father again too.

CHAPTER 24

Semira returned from school to find Mama making supper.

'I'm making everyone *tsebhi dhoro*,' said Mama. 'Graham said he wanted to try Eritrean food.'

Semira bent her head to smell the spices in the bowl. Mama's spicy chicken was her favourite. 'How was your new school, Mama?'

Mama smiled. 'It was hard. Everyone could speak some English. But it was fun. Everyone tried to help each other.'

'You'll go again?'

'Of course,' Mama said. 'We can't stay with Debbie and her family for ever. I need to be able to look after us both. I'll need to be able speak

English.'

Semira watched her mother. She had never seen her like this, smiling and humming to herself as she cooked. Maybe this was what she was like before. Maybe *The Feather Diaries* had set her free.

Graham had sent the story to the newspaper. So maybe Papa could find them again. Maybe life could change for them like it had for Patrick and Debbie.

Everyone loved Mama's chicken. Graham scraped around the bowl and begged for the recipe.

Debbie offered for Semira and Mama to come to see a film at the cinema, but Mama said they would stay at home. Debbie's family needed time together, and besides, Semira and Mama wanted their own time together too.

'Let's read the diary,' said Mama when they were alone. 'Let's hear what happens to Kitty on her adventures.'

Semira fetched the diary, curled up beside Mama on the sofa, and began to read.

Monday 3rd August, 1891

Dearest Friend,

This is the saddest day of my whole life. I realize
that I have not written a note for two months
now. Daily life has much been the same, except
for some trips to the Duchess to help write replies
to the ever-increasing members of the Society of
the Protection of Birds.

I had been longing and longing for a letter
from dear Kitty. I so wanted to hear about
lions and elephants and life in Africa. So when
Georgina Lewis came to our house this morning I
rushed down the stairs in anticipation.

But she stood in the parlour and I could see her
eyes were quite red from crying. I never thought
of her as one who suffers from nerves.

As I stepped through the door, they all turned.
Mother had a peculiar look on her face that I
couldn't quite place. Father looked quite pale.

'What is it?' I asked.

'It is your Aunt Katherine,' said Mother. 'She
is dead.'

Father sat down with his head in his hands.

It felt that I had been struck by a hammer blow. I felt my world fall away from me, and bile rise inside my throat.

'No,' I said. 'It can't be true. What makes you say such a thing?'

'I received the news only today,' said Georgie. 'Kitty and her husband died in a shipwreck. Their steamship sank in a storm. There were no survivors.'

'Are you sure?' I said.

Georgie held my hand. 'Quite sure. The news has taken a long time to come back to London. But there is no doubt.'

I closed my eyes and felt Georgie's arms around me, but it was Kitty I wanted. My Kitty. My dear, dear Kitty.

'Did you say Katherine was married?' said Mother. She couldn't hide the disgust in her voice.

'Yes,' said Georgie 'She was married to Albert Wells.'

'The stoker?' said Father.

'Indeed,' said Georgie

'She defied you Clarence,' cried Mother shrilly.

'She has embarrassed your family and brought our good name into disrepute.'

Mrs Tindall came into the room and put her hand on my shoulder. She gripped onto me, her eyes red with tears. She didn't say anything but didn't need to. I knew she felt Kitty's loss deeply too.

Everyone seemed quite shocked, except Mother who seemed more invigorated than I have seen her for years. 'We shall mourn her and then we shall never talk of her again,' said Mother. 'Maybe it is a blessing for everyone, and a good thing it has ended this way.'

I'm not sure of the exact pattern of events after that, but the bell rang again and Mrs Tindall went to the door and showed in the Duchess of Portland. Mother curtsied and became quite flustered.

The Duchess nodded and said how sorry she was for our loss.

'She was such a wilful young woman,' said Mother. 'Quite uncontrollable emotions.'

'May I talk with Henrietta, please,' said the Duchess.

Mother and Father stood there for a while, not quite understanding.

'Alone,' said the Duchess.

'Yes of course,' said Father, taking Mother by the arm and leading her out of the room.

I felt an ache burn deep in my chest. 'Is it true? Is it really true?'

The Duchess nodded.

And somehow, it was as if she confirmed it, as if it might not have been possible until then. And I began to sob. My Kitty. Dead. Gone for ever.

The Duchess held me against her and I could hear her sobs with mine.

'Such a waste,' she wept. 'A bright and brave young woman. Gone too early. She didn't even get to Cape Town. She didn't make it to Africa.'

But I know it mattered not that she didn't get to Cape Town. She was with her Albert on a grand adventure. And I hear Kitty's words as if she is here beside me. 'Oh Hen, it doesn't matter. Don't you see? We have to treasure each precious moment and hold it deep inside. We never know what might happen. We must remember to live and enjoy the glory of the ride.'

The Duchess and Georgie both left soon after that. The Duchess told me to visit her anytime, but somehow I didn't think I would. It was as if some part of me had died too. Some part of my life had just ended.

I sat in the parlour and Mrs Tindall brought me hot cocoa. I just sat there, my tears falling, feeling empty. Mrs Tindall sat with me. Maybe her hopes and dreams had died with Kitty too. The awful truth struck me that I could never speak with Kitty again, or hear her laughter, or race the wind on a bicycle with her. It was as if everything good and bright about the world had been crushed, leaving nothing but darkness.

I do not know how long I had been there, but Mother came into the room. She was wearing a long green evening gown and carrying the hat with the green bird Father had bought for her.

'Ah, Mrs Tindall,' she said. 'I was wondering where you were. I need you to set my hair. Clarence and I are going to the Elridge's and we do not want to be late. I want to look my best as the Mayor of London will be there.'

'How can you go, Mother?' I said. 'Aunt Katherine is dead.'

Mother looked at me as if I were some insolent child.

She put her hat down on the table beside me and wagged her finger. 'Katherine was an embarrassment to the good name of this family. Your father works hard to be respectable in society. This is why we are going tonight. I want you to forget your Aunt Katherine. I want you to forget all about her.'

I felt anger building up inside me. Rage spread through my chest and arms and fingers.

Mother turned to Mrs Tindall. 'Come. I need my hair to be dressed.'

I watched them leave the room.

Then my rage exploded. I could not contain it. I picked up the hat from the table where Mother had left it. I trampled it beneath my feet and tore at it with my bare hands. I bit it and kicked it until it was quite destroyed. By the time I had finished, it was a mangled mess of felt and wire.

Except for the poor bird. I couldn't bring myself to destroy the bird. It was so utterly perfect, held in a moment of flight, its beak open in some silent desperate cry as if trying to escape.

CHAPTER 25

Semira held the book against her chest. Tears were falling down her cheeks. Mama was crying too. Kitty had died over a hundred years ago, but her death felt as raw as if she had just died today.

Semira felt her loss.

It was as if the dream she had held for her father's return had gone too. If brave Kitty could die, then her father could too. Maybe there wasn't any rule in the universe that said if you were brave and honest and true, you would somehow be rewarded. People died, and that was that. Some bad people like Robel survived and some good people died. It was more likely that Papa had died crossing the desert or sea than he had made it to England. Her dream of him standing at the end of the finish line in Brighton to throw his arms around her had gone.

Patrick and his family came back from the cinema. Patrick walked into the room holding up a paper. 'We're famous, Semira,' he said. 'It's in here, the bit about looking for your dad. Graham said the paper want to come and hear your story. He said . . . '

Patrick stopped mid-sentence seeing Semira and Mama in tears.

Debbie rushed forward. 'What is it? What has happened?'

Semira held the cloth-bound diary in her hand. It seemed so silly really. How could she explain they were crying about someone who had died long, long ago?

'It's Kitty. Kitty's dead,' said Semira.

Debbie frowned. 'Who's Kitty?'

'She's a girl in a diary,' said Semira. 'The girl who writes it, well, she's a bit like me.'

Debbie kneeled down and took the diary in her hands and traced her finger down the feather. '*The Feather Diaries?*' she said. 'May I look?'

Semira nodded and watched Debbie turn the pages and read some of the entries.

'It's so old,' said Debbie.

Graham and Lily looked over her shoulder.

'Who wrote it?' asked Lily.

'A girl called Hen,' said Semira. 'But she's just found out that her friend has died.'

'Can you read it to us?' said Lily.

Semira held Mama's hand and nodded. 'I think Hen would like you to hear her story.'

And so Semira took the book back from Debbie and read on, reading in English and then translating for Mama.

But the first words of the next entry made her go cold inside.

Tuesday 4th August, 1891

Dearest Friend,

I am sorry to have to tell you, but this will be my last entry. I can never write to you again. It is simply too dangerous.

After the events of yesterday when I tore up Mother's hat, Father called upon his doctor. They said I had suffered a very bad case of the nerves and the doctor declared that I was too much for Mother to cope with.

I am lucky that they considered me too young for the madhouse, but instead Mother is sending me to stay with a great-aunt in Inverness all the way at the top of Scotland.

She says it is best for us all. How I shall miss little Lettie. How cruel this situation is. Father says my actions might cause Mother and Lettie to suffer.

'You are a worry for your mother, Henrietta,' said Father. 'You have no respect.'

'None at all,' agreed Mother. 'I blame Katherine for putting silly and dangerous ideas into your head. Why, if I had known you would be riding bicycles I would never have let you out.'

Maybe there was something in knowing I would soon be far, far away that drove me to be insolent. Or maybe it was because I didn't have any respect for Mother any more.

'You really should try cycling, Mother dear,'
I said. 'It might be a cure for your nervous
disposition.'

'Henrietta! Cycling is dangerous. Are you not
afraid of a fatal tumble?'

I glared at her then. 'I'm not afraid of dying,
Mother. I'm afraid of becoming like you. I'm
afraid of never having lived.'

'Henrietta!' Father was most angry, yet in a
strange way I was beginning to enjoy myself. I
began to realize that could be who I wanted to be
and they couldn't stop me.

Father had gone quite purple in the face. 'I
hope that in time, Henrietta, when you return to
the fold of this family and the love you have here,
you will be more obedient.'

'Your Aunt Katherine was an abomination,
Henrietta,' spat Mother. 'An abomination.'

'No, Mother,' I said. 'It is you who are the
abomination. You are worse than any man,
because while they deny us power, you deny our
will to fight for it.'

'Henrietta, go to your room,' shouted Father.
'And stay there until the carriage arrives to take

you to the train station. I hope Scotland will knock some sense into you.'

Mrs Tindall came to help me pack my bags. She wrapped up a whole cake for my journey.

'I shall miss you, Miss Henrietta,' she said.

'I shall miss you too,' I said. 'And your cake.'

'I won't ever forget your Aunt Katherine,' she said, wiping tears from her eyes.

I shook my head. 'No,' I said. 'Neither shall I.'

So tomorrow I will head up into Scotland far, far away. Mother and Father think it is somewhere I will learn my manners and have time to reflect upon my actions. But once a fire burns in your soul it is so difficult to extinguish. For I have plans. Oh dearest friend, I shall learn to choose my battles wisely. I will listen and question the world around me, and when I am older, when I am ready, I will come and fight with the courage of lions.

You will hear me roar.

For what people like Mother and Father do not realize, is that Kitty's life was never in vain. We will pass this torch from one woman to another.

We will keep it burning so brightly for each other
and for those who come after us.
So goodbye, my dear, dear friend.
Thank you for listening.
How I shall miss you.

Hen x

CHAPTER 26

Semira flicked over the pages, but the rest of them were just blank. It was as if Hen had walked out of the room never to return.

'She's gone,' said Semira, 'Gone.'

Lily stared at the pages. 'What happened to her?'

Semira frantically flipped through the pages again as if an answer would magically appear.

'Google her,' said Patrick. 'Maybe she turned out to be famous.' He logged in to the computer and typed in Henrietta Waterman, Victorian era. 'There's nothing.'

Semira walked over and looked at the screen. 'We'll never know.'

'Where did you find the diary?' asked

Patrick.

Semira frowned. 'It was in a hatbox at the market. On Ron's stall.'

'The clearance people?' said Graham.

Semira nodded. 'He said it belonged to a mad professor.'

'Do you know where the professor lives?' said Debbie.

Semira shook her head. 'Ron clears out houses after people have died.'

'Not always,' said Graham. 'Sometimes it's when people have to go into care homes.'

Patrick picked up the diary. 'Why don't we go and ask? It's worth a try.'

The next day, Semira packed up the hat and diary in the hatbox and walked with Patrick to Ron's stall.

Ron glared at them. 'I'm not taking that back,' he said. 'You bought it fair and square.'

'It's not that,' said Semira. 'We want to find the owner. You said it belonged to a professor.'

Ron frowned. 'Yeah, that's right. Mad as a box of frogs.'

'Is the Professor dead?' asked Patrick.

'Don't think so,' said Ron, scratching his chin. 'Why d'you want to know?'

'We want to return it,' said Patrick.

The woman on the next stall leaned over. 'Did the Professor live in the house on the corner of the park? Was that the house you cleared?'

Ron nodded.

'That's Prof Thomas. Same care home as my nan,' she said. 'Apparently, the Professor terrifies the staff. I'll give you the address if you like.'

Patrick turned to Semira. 'D'you want to go?'

Semira nodded and clutched the hat. As they walked, Semira had the strange feeling that two worlds were coming together.

They stopped outside the care home. It was a huge house with tall windows and a garden with a large cedar spreading its branches low over the ground. They walked up the steps and knocked on the door.

A nurse opened the door. 'Hello?'

'We've come to see Professor Thomas,' she said.

The nurse looked flustered. 'We're short-staffed today. Come back tomorrow.'

'Please,' said Patrick, 'we won't be long.'

The nurse opened the door wider and sighed. 'Through there, in the lounge. The Professor doesn't get many visitors.' The nurse's attention was distracted by a man coming down the stairs. 'Oh Mr Peach, use the handrail please.'

Semira and Patrick slipped past her into the lounge. There were elderly people in chairs around the edges of the room and a TV blaring at one end. They stared around wondering which one was the Professor.

Semira whispered, 'What d'you think he looks like?'

Patrick shrugged his shoulders.

Semira bent down beside a small bird-like woman in a chair. 'Excuse me,' said Semira. 'Can you tell me if Professor Thomas is here? We've come to see him.'

'Disappointing,' said the woman. 'Very

disappointing.'

'I'm sorry?' said Semira.

The woman glared at them. It's very disappointing that two young people in this day and age presume to think a professor is more likely to be a man than a woman.'

Patrick frowned. 'You're the Professor?'

'Yes,' said the woman sharply. 'And who are you?'

'I'm Semira,' said Semira. 'And this is Patrick.'

They both stood there in awkward silence.

'Well it's not Christmas,' said the woman, 'so I doubt you've come to sing me carols.'

'No,' said Semira.

'So what have you come for?'

Semira lifted the hat from her bag. 'We've come to bring you this. We think it belongs to you.'

The Professor's frown softened and she stared at the hat for a long time. 'Where did you find it?'

'I bought it at a stall,' said Semira.

The woman narrowed her eyes. 'Why? What

made you want to buy it?'

'It was the bird at first,' said Semira. 'It reminded me of someone I once knew. But then there was something else. A diary.'

The Professor pulled herself to her feet. 'Come, let's go to my room. Let me hear your story there.'

Patrick and Semira followed the Professor into a light-filled room that overlooked the lawns. Birds flew down to the bird feeder outside her window. Two small birds with flashes of gold on their wings and bright-red cheeks were pecking for seeds.

'Goldfinches!' said Patrick. 'My favourites.'

The Professor turned her beady eye on Patrick. 'Well it's a relief to know young people still pay some attention to the world beyond their screens.'

Semira and Patrick just stared at each other, not quite knowing what to say.

'Well, take a seat,' said the Professor. 'So, tell me how you came to find this diary and how you come to be here.'

Semira started slowly at first, but the

Professor was a good listener. She hadn't meant to mention Mama and Robel, but somehow the whole story came tumbling out. Patrick interrupted with his parts of the story too.

'We want to know what happened to Henrietta,' said Semira. She looked down at her hands. 'We need to know.'

The Professor nodded. She took the hat from Semira and stroked the green bird. 'Now it is my turn to tell you the rest of the story,' she said. She reached into a drawer next to her bed and pulled out an old photograph album.

She opened it onto the first page. A young girl stared back from a sepia photograph, a slight frown upon her face and her mouth upturned in a shy smile. She was wearing a lace cotton dress and her hair was braided into plaits.

It was dated May, 1891.

Below the photo, pencilled in neat handwriting was the name, *Henrietta Waterman.*

CHAPTER 27

Semira held the album on her lap. She couldn't take her eyes from the photograph. This was Hen. This was her friend. This was the girl who had reached through time and helped her to be strong. She felt tears well up inside her.

'What happened to her?' whispered Semira. 'Did she change the world?'

'All in good time,' said the Professor. She leaned across to hold the photograph album. 'Henrietta did indeed go to Inverness where she spent the rest of her teenage years studying and riding horses and cycling in the mountains.' The Professor turned a page to show a snowy scene with Henrietta on a pony with mountains behind her. 'She loved her time in Scotland, but her only great sadness was that her sister Lettie died from measles when she was seven and Henrietta never got to see her again.'

'How long did she stay in Scotland?' asked Semira.

'She stayed most of her life. She refused to have anything to do with her parents. When she turned eighteen she took a room with Georgina Lewis in Edinburgh and they became the greatest of friends.

'You mean the doctor?' said Semira.

The Professor nodded. 'Yes, Georgina's sister was a suffragette and Henrietta joined the movement. She married a doctor, Charles Thomas, and they had a son they named Albert. Henrietta never led the suffragette movement but she was always there, working tirelessly behind the scenes. She and her husband did much work to help the welfare of people in the lunatic asylums too.' The Professor turned the page to show a photograph of Hen as a young woman riding a bicycle, balancing a small boy on the handlebars. She was laughing into the camera.

'She's wearing breeches,' said Semira.

'Oh yes,' said the Professor. 'There were big changes happening in the world. Women were needed for all sorts of jobs as men were away at war. Her son, Albert, was my father. He was badly injured during World War Two. He suffered dreadful shell shock, and the way he coped with it was to walk for hours across the hills watching birds. He said they gave him peace knowing there was so much beauty still to be seen in a cruel world. He gave me his love of wild things and wild places too.'

'Are you a twitcher?' asked Patrick.

'Sort of, I suppose,' said the Professor. 'It's been my life. I studied zoology and went on to research birds in far-flung places. I ended up doing research for the RSPB. It's strange to think that my grandmother was there at the very first meeting.'

'So did Henrietta leave you the hat?' said Semira.

'No,' said the Professor. 'Sadly Henrietta died when Albert was a child and contact with the family had been lost.'

Semira turned back to the first photograph of Hen when she was twelve. It seemed strange to think that at the time of writing, her whole life stretched out before her. 'So how did you find the diary and the hat?'

'They found me,' said the Professor. I had just become a professor and moved into a new flat in London when there was a knock at the door. There was an elderly lady carrying a hatbox. She said she had tracked me down and believed I was the owner of the hat.'

'Who was she?' said Patrick.

Professor Thomas smiled. 'It was Mrs Tindall's daughter. The hat had been kept in the family.'

'The housekeeper?' said Semira.

'The same one,' said the Professor. 'Mrs Tindall found Hen's diary and kept it safe. She kept the hat Henrietta destroyed too. She never got a chance to return it to her.'

'Why would Mrs Tindall keep the hat?' said

Semira. 'It was ruined.'

'This might explain,' said the Professor. She reached into the drawers again and pulled out a small white cardboard box. It looked yellowed with age and stained with grease.

Semira opened it up and looked inside. It was empty except for lots and lots of names written in pencil in very small, neat handwriting. Semira tried to read them. They were all names of women.

The Professor smiled. 'Do you remember Mrs Tindall and her cake in the diary?'

'Yes,' said Semira. 'She was always baking.'

The Professor closed the cake box. 'And do you remember how she always sent Kitty home with cake?'

'Yes,' said Semira. She thought back to the times Mrs Tindall and Kitty seemed to share a secret look.

'Well,' said the Professor, 'Kitty was a bit ahead of her time. The suffragette movement hadn't really got going. But Kitty was trying to organize mass protests by women. Mrs Tindall had a secret network of women interested in joining together. She wrote down the names of those interested in the movement and passed them on to Kitty inside a cake box every time they met. She hoped Kitty would lead the movement.'

Semira laughed. 'Mrs Tindall and her cake! I never guessed!'

The Professor nodded. 'There were many ready to fight for the cause.' She picked up the hat and ran her hands across it. 'Mrs Tindall saw the ruined hat as an ultimate act of defiance. I kept it with me as a reminder all this time, until I collapsed and was taken to hospital a month ago. I was devastated to think the hat and the diary had been taken. The clearance people had thought it was just rubbish. When I asked for it back, they said it had been sold. I thought it had been lost for ever.'

'Well it's back.' Semira smiled. 'It's yours again now.'

The Professor pushed the hat and diary back into Semira's hands. 'I have no children of my own. Henrietta and Kitty's stories have become your story too. You keep them, Semira.

Never forget them and what they did.
Take the torch and hold it high.
Let it burn brightly.
And pass it on.'

CHAPTER 28

Semira did the final checks. She lubricated the chain, tightened the brakes, and checked the gears.

It was the day of the ride. Debbie had pulled out because of an old knee injury and so she and Mama said they would drive ahead to Brighton to wait at the finish line.

Mama watched Semira as she wiped down the paintwork. Semira had painted her bicycle frame in the red, yellow, green, and blue of the Eritrean flag.

'It looks good,' said Mama. She crouched next to Semira, placing her old carpetbag on the ground beside the bike. 'Semira, there is something I want you to have.'

Semira glanced at the carpetbag. It was old and ragged and had a musty smell. She knew how fond Mama was of it and didn't want to upset her.

'Mama, I can't carry that bag with me, I have no room.'

Mama laughed. 'Not the bag. Here, pass me those scissors.'

Semira picked up the scissors from the work surface and watched as her mother slipped the blade into the lining of the bag. 'Mama what are you doing?'

'I have carried this a long, long time,' she said. 'Now I think it belongs to you.'

Semira watched as her mother pulled something hidden in the lining of the bag. It was material in the colours of the Eritrean flag. Mama pulled it out and held it up. It was a large cycle shirt with the words Isaac Soloman written on the back.

'It was your father's,' said Mama. 'I needed to have something of his when I left. I have kept it hidden all this time. I think he would have liked for you to have this now.'

Semira held the shirt in her hands and buried her nose in the material, trying to inhale the smell of him.

'Put it on,' said Mama. 'Here, let me help you.'

Semira pulled the shirt on. It was too big for her, but she didn't mind. She didn't mind one single bit.

Mama held her at arm's length and smiled. 'He would be so proud if he could see you now.'

Semira blinked back tears.

'Have you given your bike a name yet?' said Lily. 'You need to have a name before the ride.'

'I have,' smiled Semira.

'What is it?'

Semira ran her hands along the crossbar. 'She's called Glory.'

'Why Glory?' asked Lily.

Semira smiled and shrugged her shoulders. 'She just is. After something someone once said.'

Semira helped to lift the bicycles onto the bike carrier on the car and checked her bag for puncture repair kit, water bottles, and food.

Patrick strapped the bikes down. 'Did you know you're famous?'

Semira looked at him. 'What are you talking about?'

'The photo we sent; it's been shared right across Twitter and Facebook.'

'How?' said Semira.

'Graham's cycle club put the article on their website. It's been shared over five thousand times, the last time I looked.'

Semira climbed into the car next to Patrick, while Lily sat in the front. Semira stared out at the streets and houses as they whizzed by. Maybe her father would see the photo. Maybe someone who knew him had seen it and told him. Was it too impossible to hope for? Could he be waiting at the finish line for her?

'Not far now to the start line,' said Graham. 'This is Haywards Heath.'

Semira pressed her face against the window as they passed the railway station, and the coffee shops, and burger bars. She tried to imagine Kitty pushing her bike along the dirt tracks and meeting Albert here among the steam engines and smell of coal. She imagined Kitty in her tweed jacket and breeches and flat cap. Did places have memories? It was strange to think *The Feather Diaries* had unlocked a window into the past.

Graham parked the car and they unloaded the bikes. Already there were people lined up and ready up at the start line.

'Ready?' said Graham. 'Remember, it's not a race.'

At the sound of the starting hooter, Semira pushed off, moving slowly at first in the mass of bicycles. She managed to follow Patrick out to the front of the line, weaving through other cyclists. She tried to imagine how her father felt when he raced, how he must have felt the power to be free. The first hill separated the pack of cyclists and Semira and Patrick soon found themselves out on their own. Semira glanced behind, but couldn't see Graham or Lily.

The miles rolled beneath them, past fields and towns. The sky was pale blue, and puffy clouds floated overhead. She let herself dream again, about Papa being there at the end of the race. She imagined him standing there, watching her cross the line in his Olympic shirt. He would open his arms wide and she would drop the bike and run into them. She had imagined it so often that it seemed to be real. Could there really be a happy ending?

As they rose to the top of a hill, the sea lay in the distance, glittering in the sunshine. A salt breeze cooled their faces.

'Not far now,' yelled Patrick.

Semira went ahead, freewheeling down the hill, towards the hope of seeing her father.

'Race you,' Patrick yelled, whizzing past.

Semira pushed hard on the pedals and caught up with him.

Soon they were flying along, side by side, the wind whistling past them, with the hot sun above and the earth blurring beneath their wheels.

'Woohoooooo!' yelled Semira. 'Woooo hoooooo!'

Patrick lifted his head back too. 'Wooooo

hoooooo!'

And in that moment, Semira understood what Kitty had meant all those years ago. There are no endings or beginnings. Life is full of moments, each one to be held as precious as the last. And she would hold this one amazing moment with its infinite possibilities. She would hold it deep inside.

It felt as if Hen and Kitty were flying alongside her. She could almost hear Kitty's voice ringing out loud.

Life is such a grand adventure. We must remember to live every moment and enjoy the glory of the ride.

Acknowledgements;

I'm indebted to the wonderful team at Oxford University Press for helping to pull the ideas of this story onto the printed page. Huge thanks to members of the Network of Eritrean Women UK for their thoughts and interesting discussions, and I hope I have managed to give Semira an authentic voice. Thanks too to the founding members of the RSPB who, all those years ago, gave a voice to the plight of birds killed for fashion.

Finally, a heartfelt thank you to my family for all the continued support.

Gill Lewis spent much of her childhood in the garden where she ran a small zoo and a veterinary hospital for creepy-crawlies, mice, and birds. When she grew up she became a real vet and travelled from the Arctic to Africa in search of interesting animals and places.

Gill now writes books for children. Her previous novels have published to worldwide critical acclaim and have been translated into more than twenty languages.

She lives in the depths of Somerset with her husband and three children and writes from a tree house in the company of squirrels.

Here are some other stories we think you'll love ...

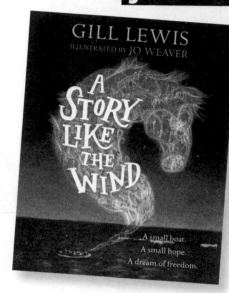

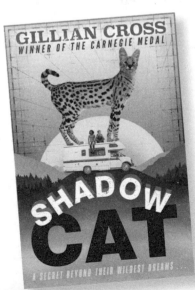

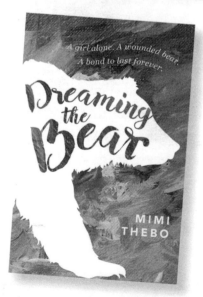